My Little Pony
Friends Forever

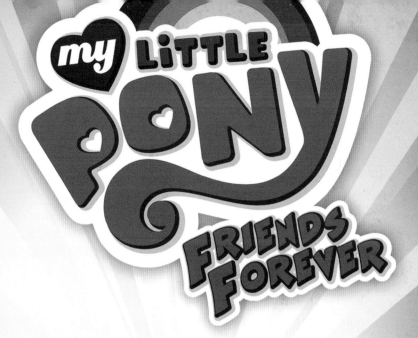

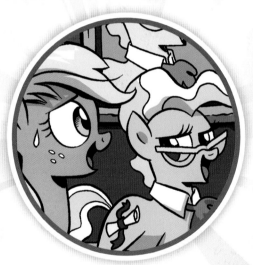

Applejack & Mayor Mare

Written by
Bobby Curnow
Art by
Brenda Hickey
Colors by
Heather Breckel
Lettered by
Neil Uyetake

ABDO Spotlight
IDW

ABDOPUBLISHING.COM

Reinforced library bound edition published in 2019 by Spotlight,
a division of ABDO, PO Box 398166, Minneapolis, Minnesota 55439.
Spotlight produces high-quality reinforced library bound editions for
schools and libraries. Published by agreement with IDW.

Printed in the United States of America, North Mankato, Minnesota.
042018
092018

THIS BOOK CONTAINS
RECYCLED MATERIALS

Licensed By:

Library of Congress Control Number: 2017961138

Publisher's Cataloging in Publication Data

Names: Curnow, Bobby, author. | Hickey, Brenda; Breckel, Heather; Uyetake,
    Neil, illustrators.
Title: Applejack & Mayor Mare / by Bobby Curnow; illustrated by Brenda
    Hickey, Heather Breckel and Neil Uyetake.
Description: Minneapolis, MN : Spotlight, 2019 | Series: My little pony:
    friends forever set 2
Summary: Applejack spends the day with Mayor Mare in hopes of clearing a
    citation on her family farm.
Identifiers: ISBN 9781532142345 (lib. bdg.)
Subjects: LCSH: My Little Pony (Trademark)--Juvenile fiction. | Mayor--
    Juvenile fiction. | Farm life--Juvenile fiction. | Citation of legal
    authorities--Juvenile fiction. | Comic books, strips, etc.--Juvenile fiction.
Classification: DDC 741.5--dc23

Spotlight

A Division of ABDO
abdopublishing.com

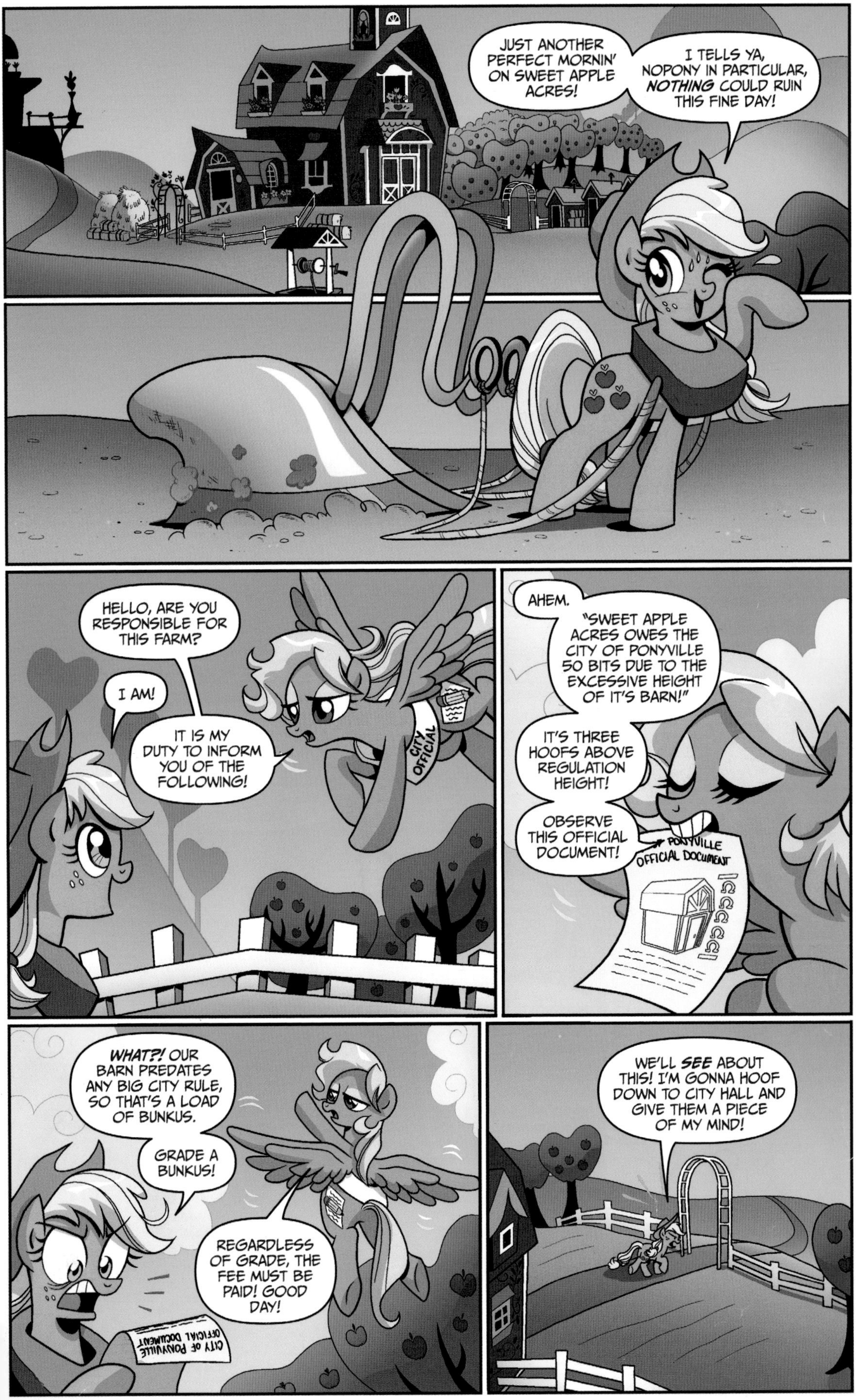
JUST ANOTHER PERFECT MORNIN' ON SWEET APPLE ACRES!
I TELLS YA, NOPONY IN PARTICULAR, NOTHING COULD RUIN THIS FINE DAY!
HELLO, ARE YOU RESPONSIBLE FOR THIS FARM?
I AM!
IT IS MY DUTY TO INFORM YOU OF THE FOLLOWING!
CITY OFFICIAL
AHEM.
"SWEET APPLE ACRES OWES THE CITY OF PONYVILLE 50 BITS DUE TO THE EXCESSIVE HEIGHT OF IT'S BARN!"
IT'S THREE HOOFS ABOVE REGULATION HEIGHT!
OBSERVE THIS OFFICIAL DOCUMENT!
PONYVILLE OFFICIAL DOCUMENT
WHAT?! OUR BARN PREDATES ANY BIG CITY RULE, SO THAT'S A LOAD OF BUNKUS.
GRADE A BUNKUS!
REGARDLESS OF GRADE, THE FEE MUST BE PAID! GOOD DAY!
CITY OF PONYVILLE OFFICIAL DOCUMENT
WE'LL SEE ABOUT THIS! I'M GONNA HOOF DOWN TO CITY HALL AND GIVE THEM A PIECE OF MY MIND!

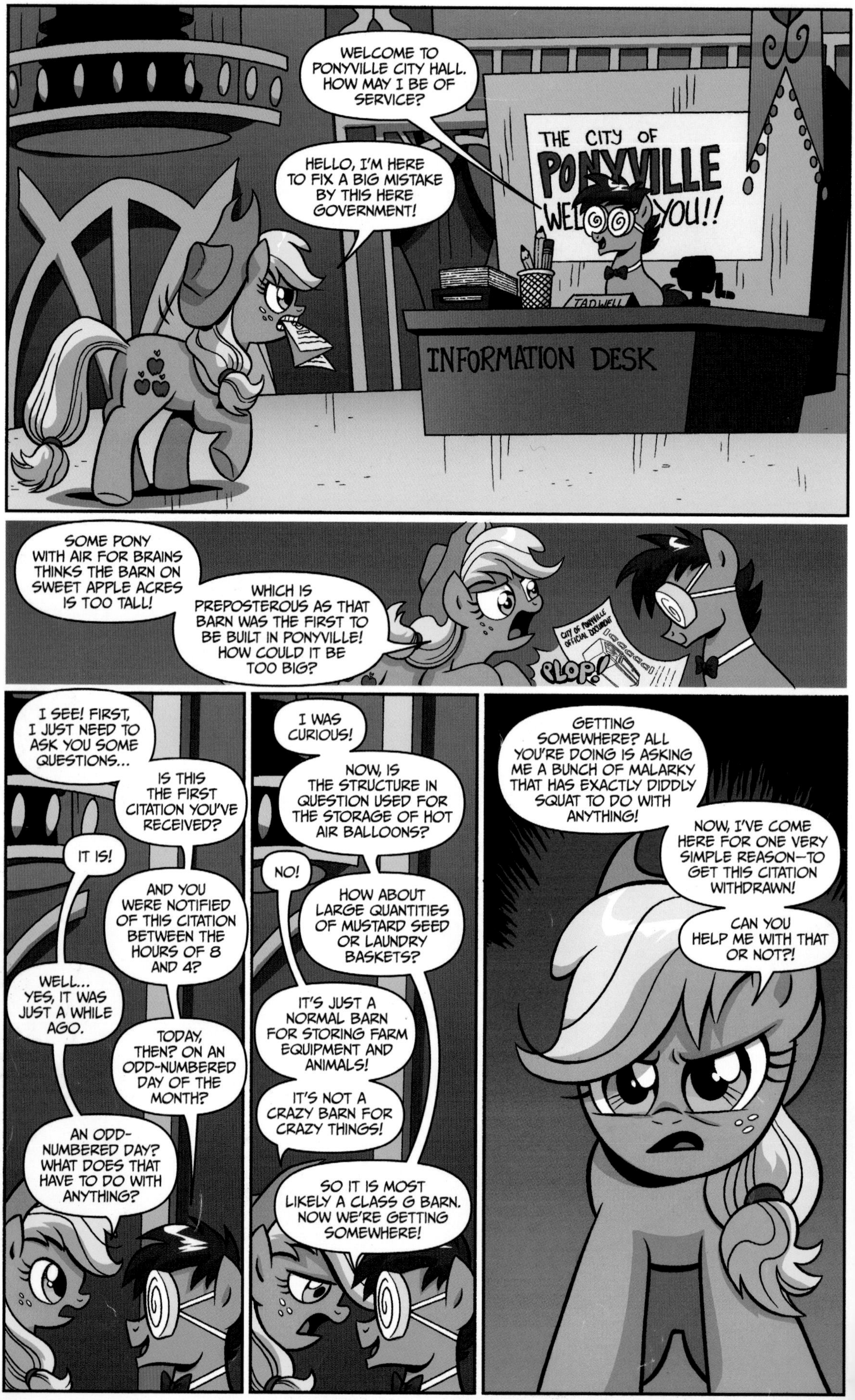
WELCOME TO PONYVILLE CITY HALL. HOW MAY I BE OF SERVICE?
HELLO, I'M HERE TO FIX A BIG MISTAKE BY THIS HERE GOVERNMENT!
THE CITY OF PONYVILLE WEL YOU!!
TADWELL
INFORMATION DESK
SOME PONY WITH AIR FOR BRAINS THINKS THE BARN ON SWEET APPLE ACRES IS TOO TALL!
WHICH IS PREPOSTEROUS AS THAT BARN WAS THE FIRST TO BE BUILT IN PONYVILLE! HOW COULD IT BE TOO BIG?
CITY OF PONYVILLE OFFICIAL DOCUMENT
PLOP!
I SEE! FIRST, I JUST NEED TO ASK YOU SOME QUESTIONS...
IS THIS THE FIRST CITATION YOU'VE RECEIVED?
IT IS!
AND YOU WERE NOTIFIED OF THIS CITATION BETWEEN THE HOURS OF 8 AND 4?
WELL... YES, IT WAS JUST A WHILE AGO.
TODAY, THEN? ON AN ODD-NUMBERED DAY OF THE MONTH?
AN ODD-NUMBERED DAY? WHAT DOES THAT HAVE TO DO WITH ANYTHING?
I WAS CURIOUS!
NOW, IS THE STRUCTURE IN QUESTION USED FOR THE STORAGE OF HOT AIR BALLOONS?
NO!
HOW ABOUT LARGE QUANTITIES OF MUSTARD SEED OR LAUNDRY BASKETS?
IT'S JUST A NORMAL BARN FOR STORING FARM EQUIPMENT AND ANIMALS!
IT'S NOT A CRAZY BARN FOR CRAZY THINGS!
SO IT IS MOST LIKELY A CLASS G BARN. NOW WE'RE GETTING SOMEWHERE!
GETTING SOMEWHERE? ALL YOU'RE DOING IS ASKING ME A BUNCH OF MALARKY THAT HAS EXACTLY DIDDLY SQUAT TO DO WITH ANYTHING!
NOW, I'VE COME HERE FOR ONE VERY SIMPLE REASON—TO GET THIS CITATION WITHDRAWN!
CAN YOU HELP ME WITH THAT OR NOT?!

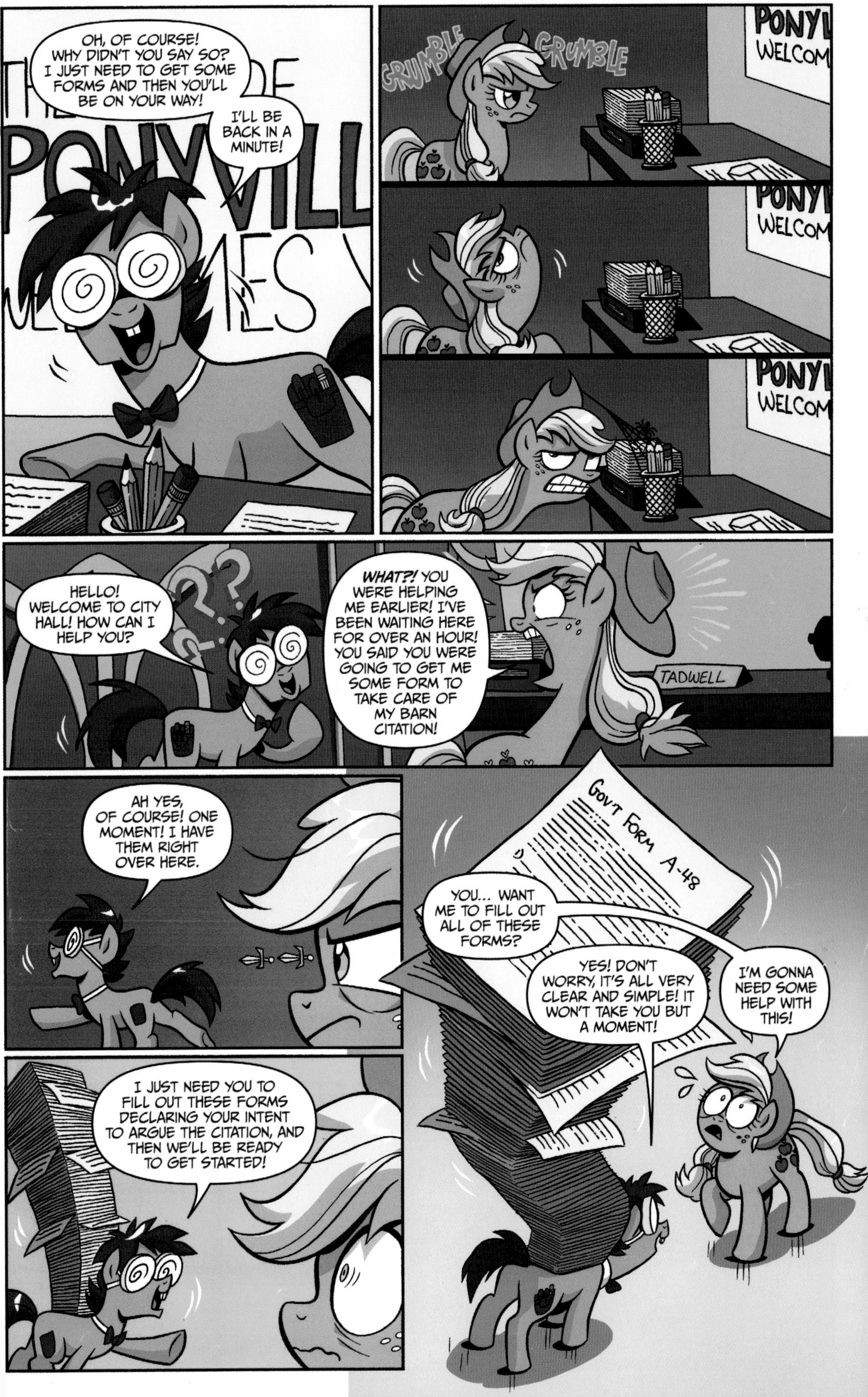

OH, OF COURSE! WHY DIDN'T YOU SAY SO? I JUST NEED TO GET SOME FORMS AND THEN YOU'LL BE ON YOUR WAY!
I'LL BE BACK IN A MINUTE!
GRUMBLE GRUMBLE
HELLO! WELCOME TO CITY HALL! HOW CAN I HELP YOU?
WHAT?! YOU WERE HELPING ME EARLIER! I'VE BEEN WAITING HERE FOR OVER AN HOUR! YOU SAID YOU WERE GOING TO GET ME SOME FORM TO TAKE CARE OF MY BARN CITATION!
TADWELL
AH YES, OF COURSE! ONE MOMENT! I HAVE THEM RIGHT OVER HERE.
I JUST NEED YOU TO FILL OUT THESE FORMS DECLARING YOUR INTENT TO ARGUE THE CITATION, AND THEN WE'LL BE READY TO GET STARTED!
GOV'T FORM A-48
YOU... WANT ME TO FILL OUT ALL OF THESE FORMS?
YES! DON'T WORRY, IT'S ALL VERY CLEAR AND SIMPLE! IT WON'T TAKE YOU BUT A MOMENT!
I'M GONNA NEED SOME HELP WITH THIS!

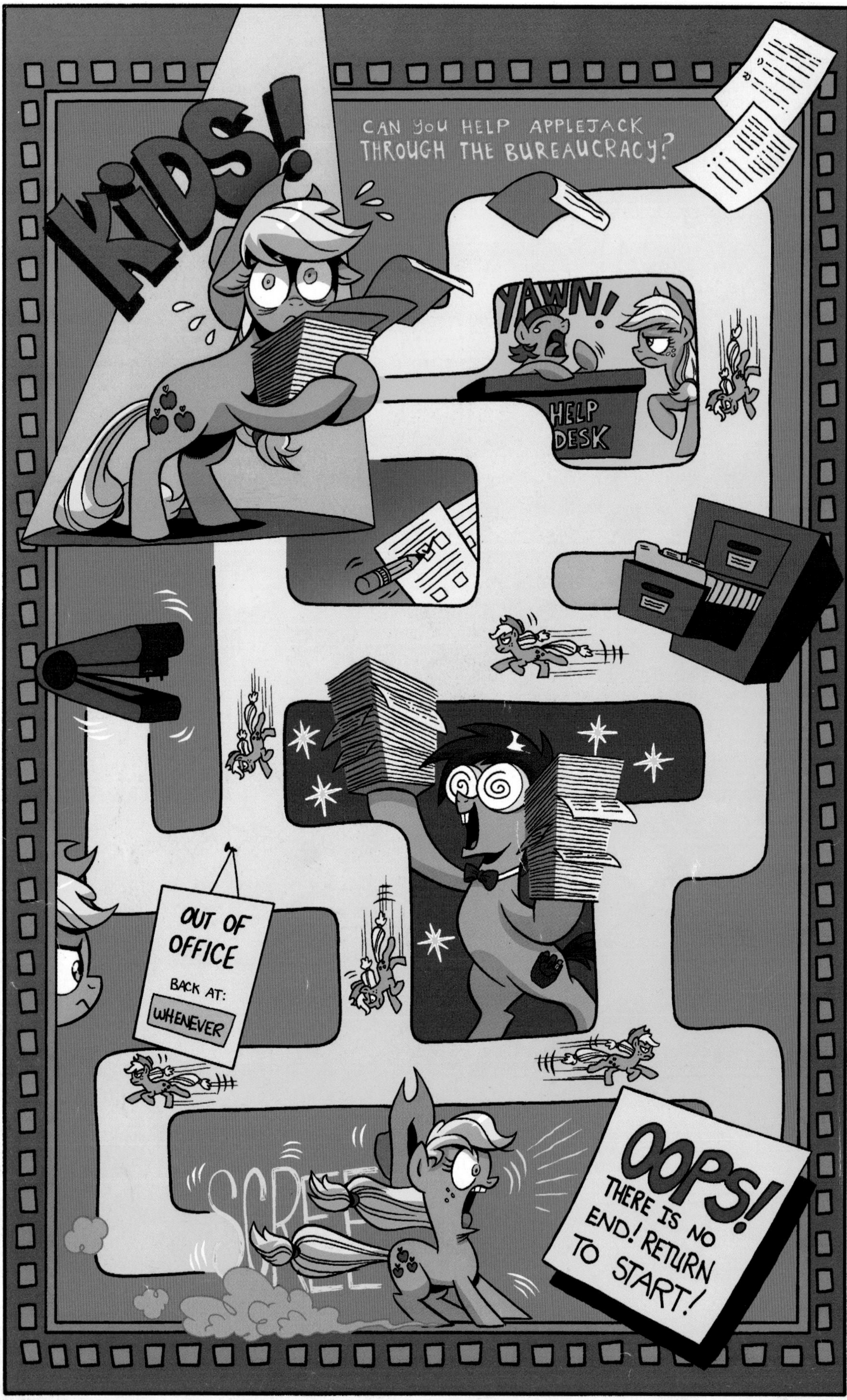

KIDS!
CAN YOU HELP APPLEJACK THROUGH THE BUREAUCRACY?
YAWN!
HELP DESK
OUT OF OFFICE
BACK AT:
WHENEVER
SCREEE
OOPS! THERE IS NO END! RETURN TO START!

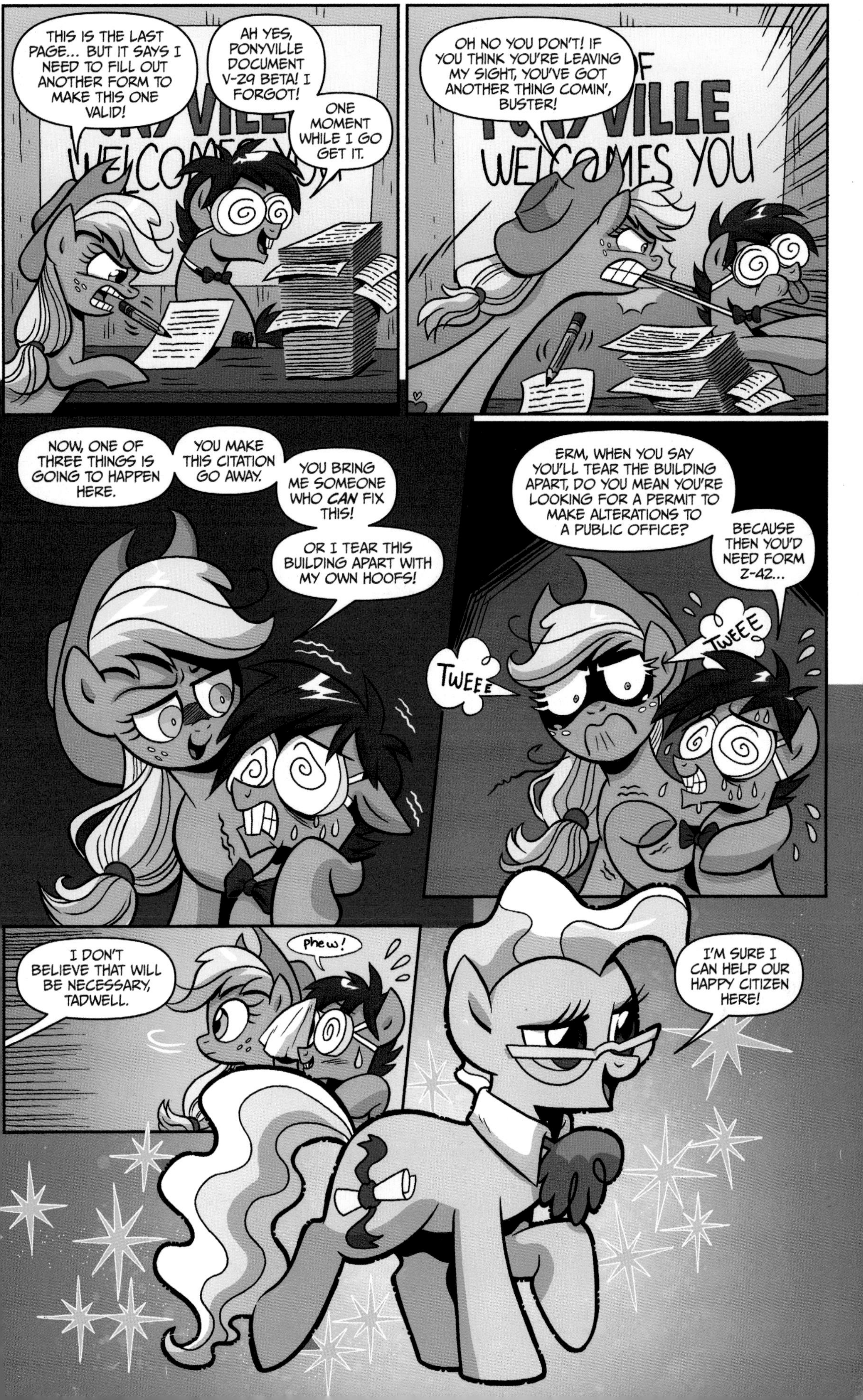

THIS IS THE LAST PAGE... BUT IT SAYS I NEED TO FILL OUT ANOTHER FORM TO MAKE THIS ONE VALID!
AH YES, PONYVILLE DOCUMENT V-29 BETA! I FORGOT!
ONE MOMENT WHILE I GO GET IT.
OH NO YOU DON'T! IF YOU THINK YOU'RE LEAVING MY SIGHT, YOU'VE GOT ANOTHER THING COMIN', BUSTER!
NOW, ONE OF THREE THINGS IS GOING TO HAPPEN HERE.
YOU MAKE THIS CITATION GO AWAY.
YOU BRING ME SOMEONE WHO *CAN* FIX THIS!
OR I TEAR THIS BUILDING APART WITH MY OWN HOOFS!
ERM, WHEN YOU SAY YOU'LL TEAR THE BUILDING APART, DO YOU MEAN YOU'RE LOOKING FOR A PERMIT TO MAKE ALTERATIONS TO A PUBLIC OFFICE?
BECAUSE THEN YOU'D NEED FORM Z-42...
TWEEE
TWEEE
I DON'T BELIEVE THAT WILL BE NECESSARY, TADWELL.
phew!
I'M SURE I CAN HELP OUR HAPPY CITIZEN HERE!

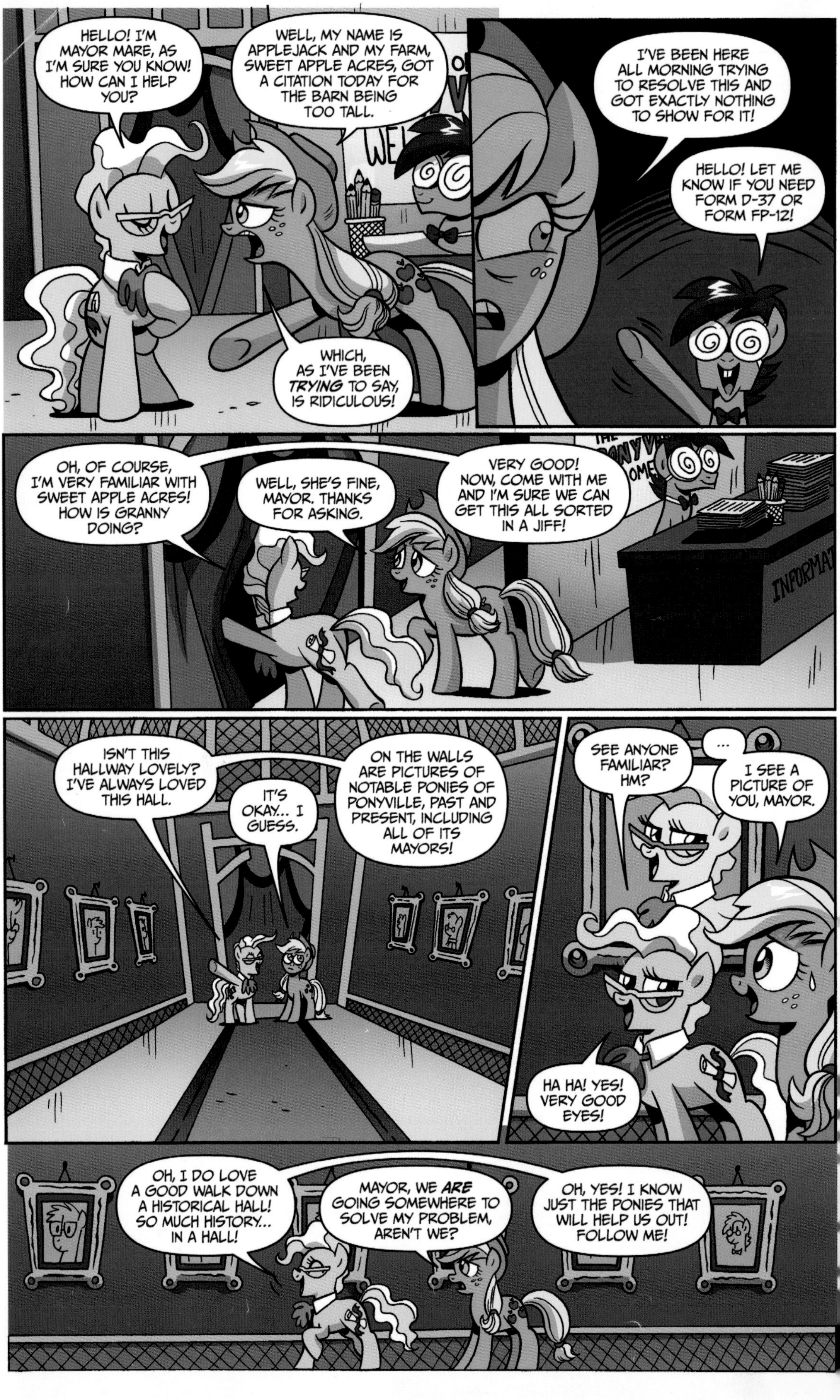
HELLO! I'M MAYOR MARE, AS I'M SURE YOU KNOW! HOW CAN I HELP YOU?
WELL, MY NAME IS APPLEJACK AND MY FARM, SWEET APPLE ACRES, GOT A CITATION TODAY FOR THE BARN BEING TOO TALL.
WHICH, AS I'VE BEEN *TRYING* TO SAY, IS RIDICULOUS!
I'VE BEEN HERE ALL MORNING TRYING TO RESOLVE THIS AND GOT EXACTLY NOTHING TO SHOW FOR IT!
HELLO! LET ME KNOW IF YOU NEED FORM D-37 OR FORM FP-12!
OH, OF COURSE, I'M VERY FAMILIAR WITH SWEET APPLE ACRES! HOW IS GRANNY DOING?
WELL, SHE'S FINE, MAYOR. THANKS FOR ASKING.
VERY GOOD! NOW, COME WITH ME AND I'M SURE WE CAN GET THIS ALL SORTED IN A JIFF!
INFORMAT
ISN'T THIS HALLWAY LOVELY? I'VE ALWAYS LOVED THIS HALL.
IT'S OKAY... I GUESS.
ON THE WALLS ARE PICTURES OF NOTABLE PONIES OF PONYVILLE, PAST AND PRESENT, INCLUDING ALL OF ITS MAYORS!
SEE ANYONE FAMILIAR? HM?
...
I SEE A PICTURE OF YOU, MAYOR.
HA HA! YES! VERY GOOD EYES!
OH, I DO LOVE A GOOD WALK DOWN A HISTORICAL HALL! SO MUCH HISTORY... IN A HALL!
MAYOR, WE *ARE* GOING SOMEWHERE TO SOLVE MY PROBLEM, AREN'T WE?
OH, YES! I KNOW JUST THE PONIES THAT WILL HELP US OUT! FOLLOW ME!

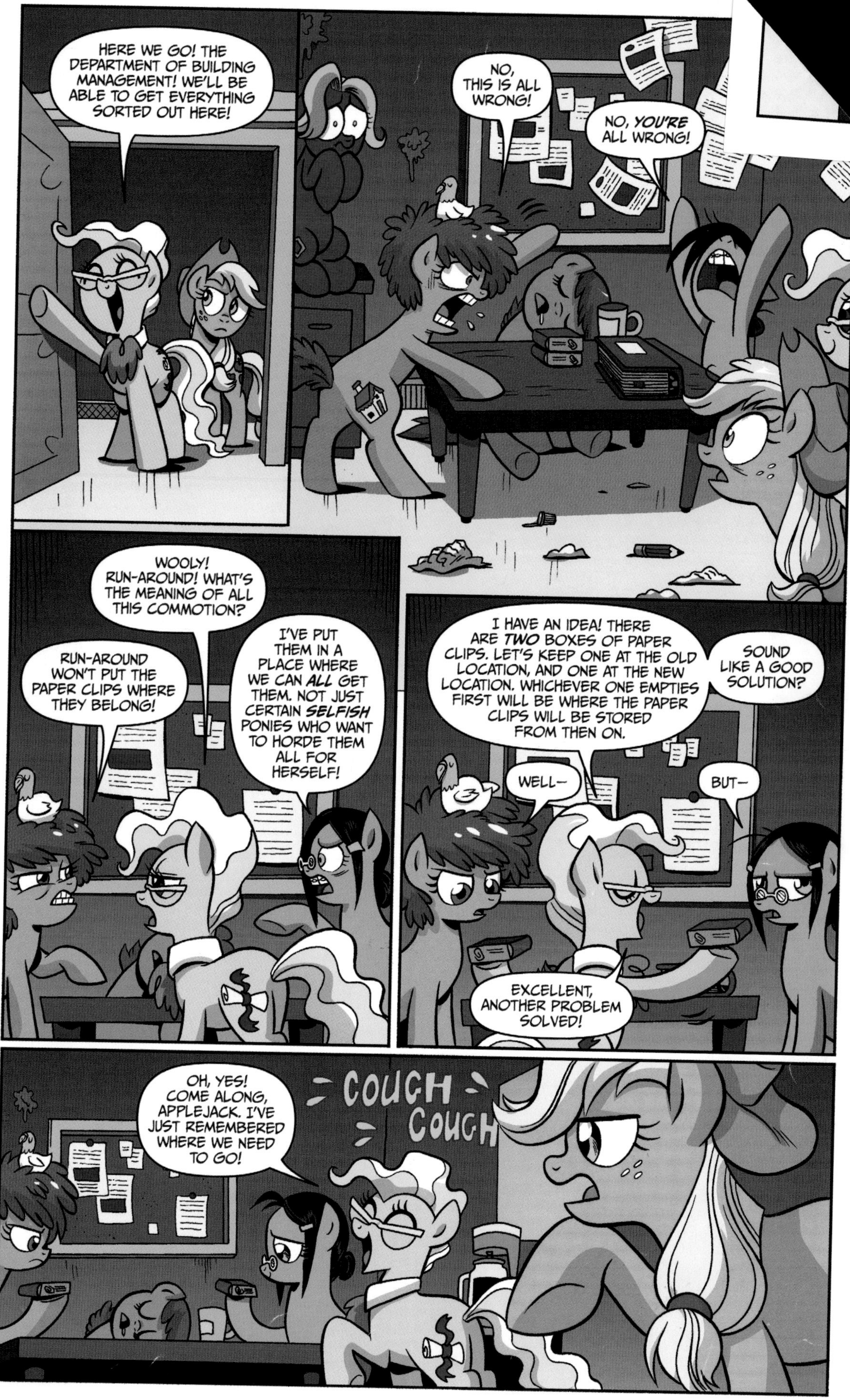
HERE WE GO! THE DEPARTMENT OF BUILDING MANAGEMENT! WE'LL BE ABLE TO GET EVERYTHING SORTED OUT HERE!
NO, THIS IS ALL WRONG!
NO, YOU'RE ALL WRONG!
WOOLY! RUN-AROUND! WHAT'S THE MEANING OF ALL THIS COMMOTION?
RUN-AROUND WON'T PUT THE PAPER CLIPS WHERE THEY BELONG!
I'VE PUT THEM IN A PLACE WHERE WE CAN ALL GET THEM. NOT JUST CERTAIN SELFISH PONIES WHO WANT TO HORDE THEM ALL FOR HERSELF!
I HAVE AN IDEA! THERE ARE TWO BOXES OF PAPER CLIPS. LET'S KEEP ONE AT THE OLD LOCATION, AND ONE AT THE NEW LOCATION. WHICHEVER ONE EMPTIES FIRST WILL BE WHERE THE PAPER CLIPS WILL BE STORED FROM THEN ON.
SOUND LIKE A GOOD SOLUTION?
WELL–
BUT–
EXCELLENT, ANOTHER PROBLEM SOLVED!
OH, YES! COME ALONG, APPLEJACK. I'VE JUST REMEMBERED WHERE WE NEED TO GO!
COUGH
COUGH

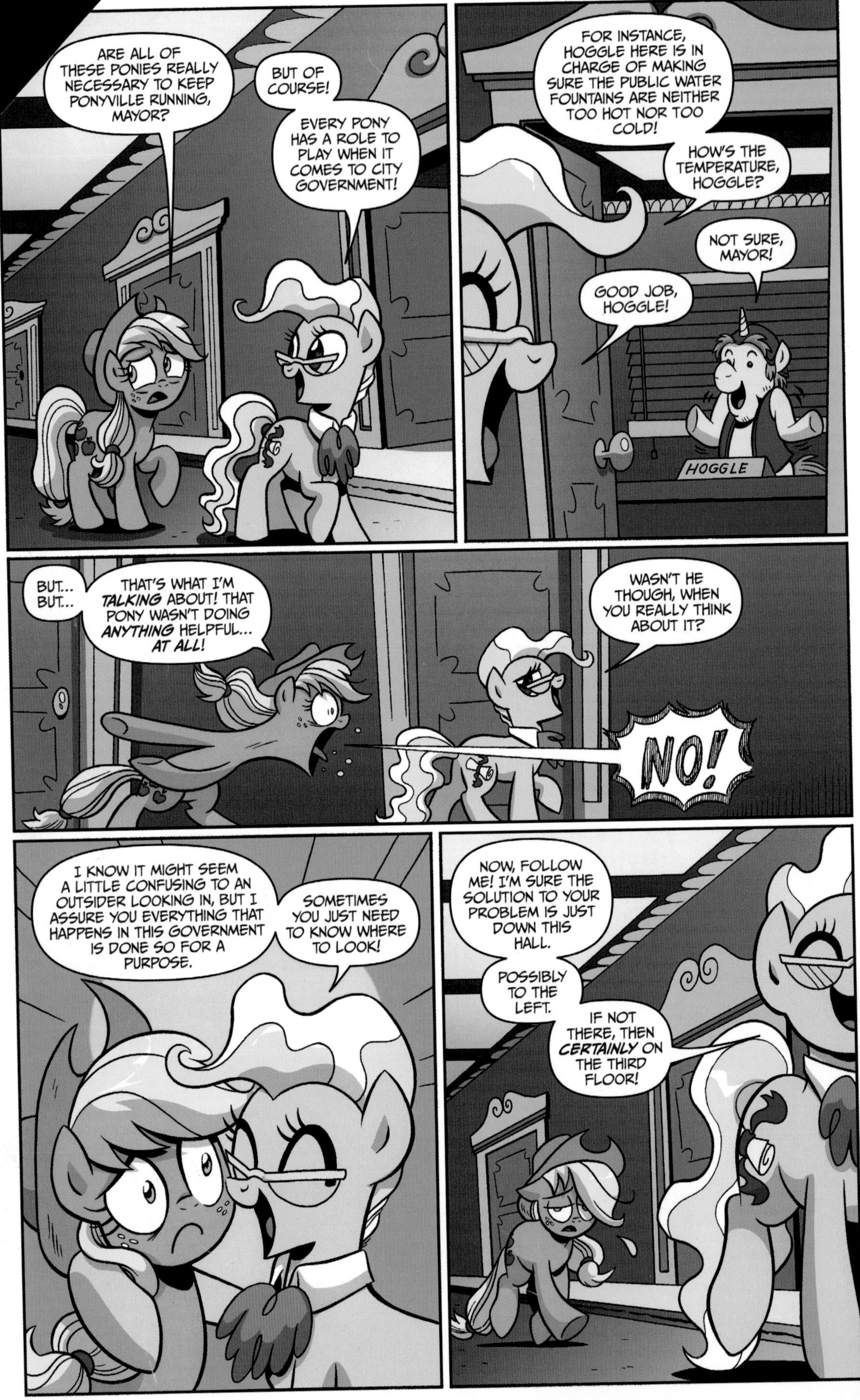
ARE ALL OF THESE PONIES REALLY NECESSARY TO KEEP PONYVILLE RUNNING, MAYOR?
BUT OF COURSE!
EVERY PONY HAS A ROLE TO PLAY WHEN IT COMES TO CITY GOVERNMENT!
FOR INSTANCE, HOGGLE HERE IS IN CHARGE OF MAKING SURE THE PUBLIC WATER FOUNTAINS ARE NEITHER TOO HOT NOR TOO COLD!
HOW'S THE TEMPERATURE, HOGGLE?
NOT SURE, MAYOR!
GOOD JOB, HOGGLE!
HOGGLE
BUT... BUT...
THAT'S WHAT I'M *TALKING* ABOUT! THAT PONY WASN'T DOING *ANYTHING* HELPFUL... *AT ALL*!
WASN'T HE THOUGH, WHEN YOU REALLY THINK ABOUT IT?
NO!
I KNOW IT MIGHT SEEM A LITTLE CONFUSING TO AN OUTSIDER LOOKING IN, BUT I ASSURE YOU EVERYTHING THAT HAPPENS IN THIS GOVERNMENT IS DONE SO FOR A PURPOSE.
SOMETIMES YOU JUST NEED TO KNOW WHERE TO LOOK!
NOW, FOLLOW ME! I'M SURE THE SOLUTION TO YOUR PROBLEM IS JUST DOWN THIS HALL.
POSSIBLY TO THE LEFT.
IF NOT THERE, THEN *CERTAINLY* ON THE THIRD FLOOR!

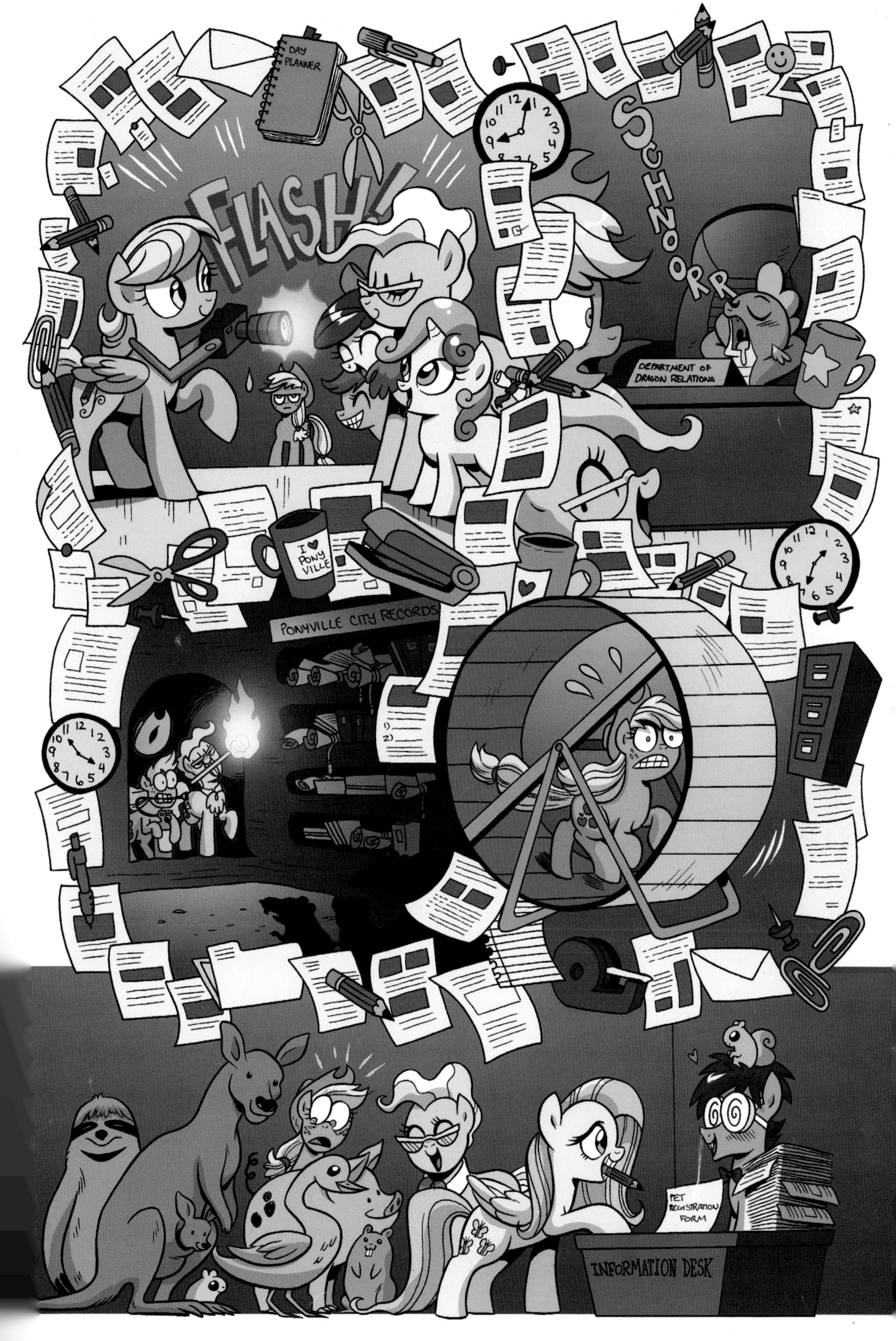
DAY PLANNER
FLASH!
SCHNOORR
DEPARTMENT OF DRAGON RELATIONS
I ♥ PONY VILLE
PONYVILLE CITY RECORDS
PET REGISTRATION FORM
INFORMATION DESK

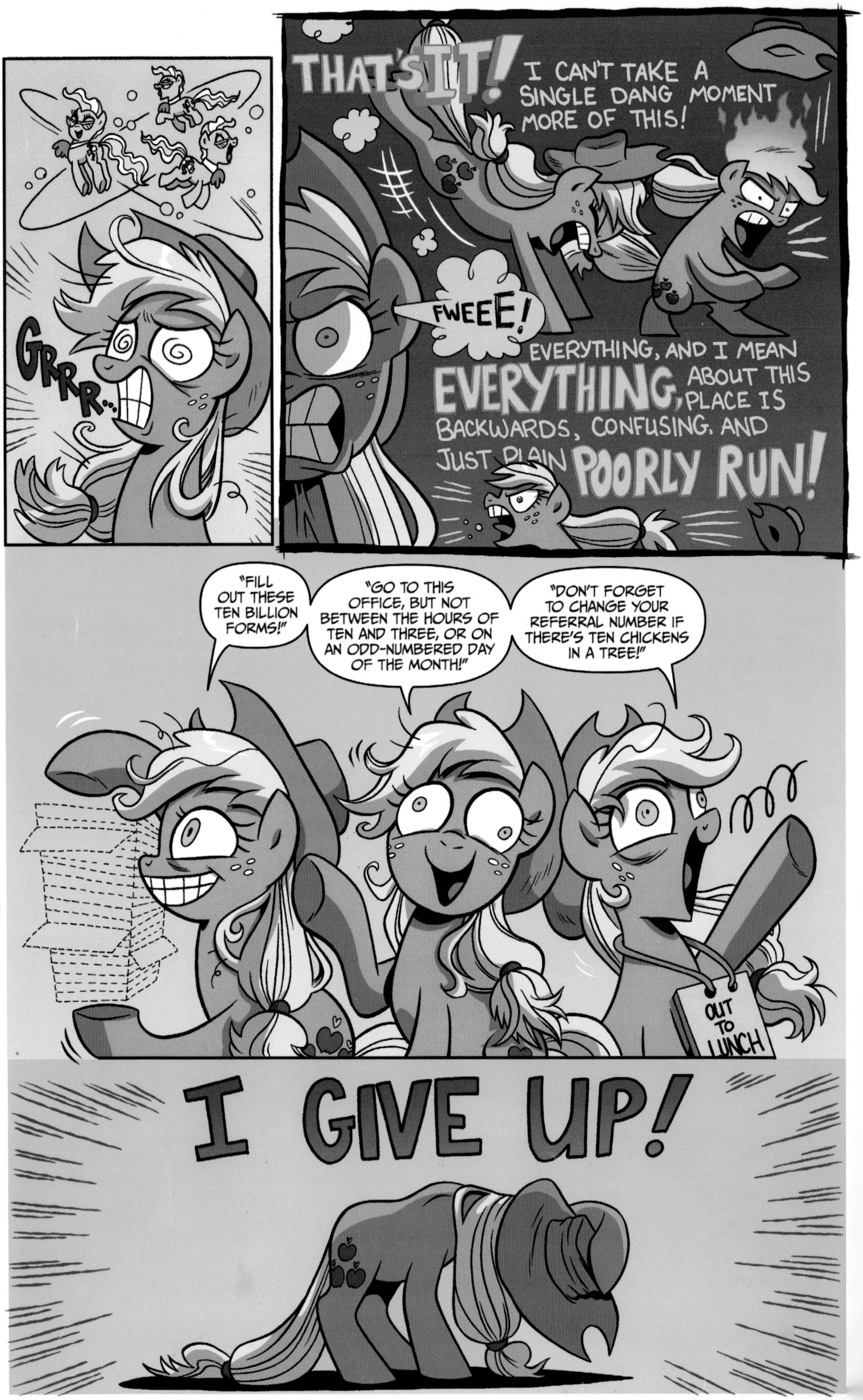
GRRRR...
THAT'S IT! I CAN'T TAKE A SINGLE DANG MOMENT MORE OF THIS!
FWEEEE!
EVERYTHING, AND I MEAN EVERYTHING, ABOUT THIS PLACE IS BACKWARDS, CONFUSING, AND JUST PLAIN POORLY RUN!
"FILL OUT THESE TEN BILLION FORMS!"
"GO TO THIS OFFICE, BUT NOT BETWEEN THE HOURS OF TEN AND THREE, OR ON AN ODD-NUMBERED DAY OF THE MONTH!"
"DON'T FORGET TO CHANGE YOUR REFERRAL NUMBER IF THERE'S TEN CHICKENS IN A TREE!"
OUT TO LUNCH
I GIVE UP!

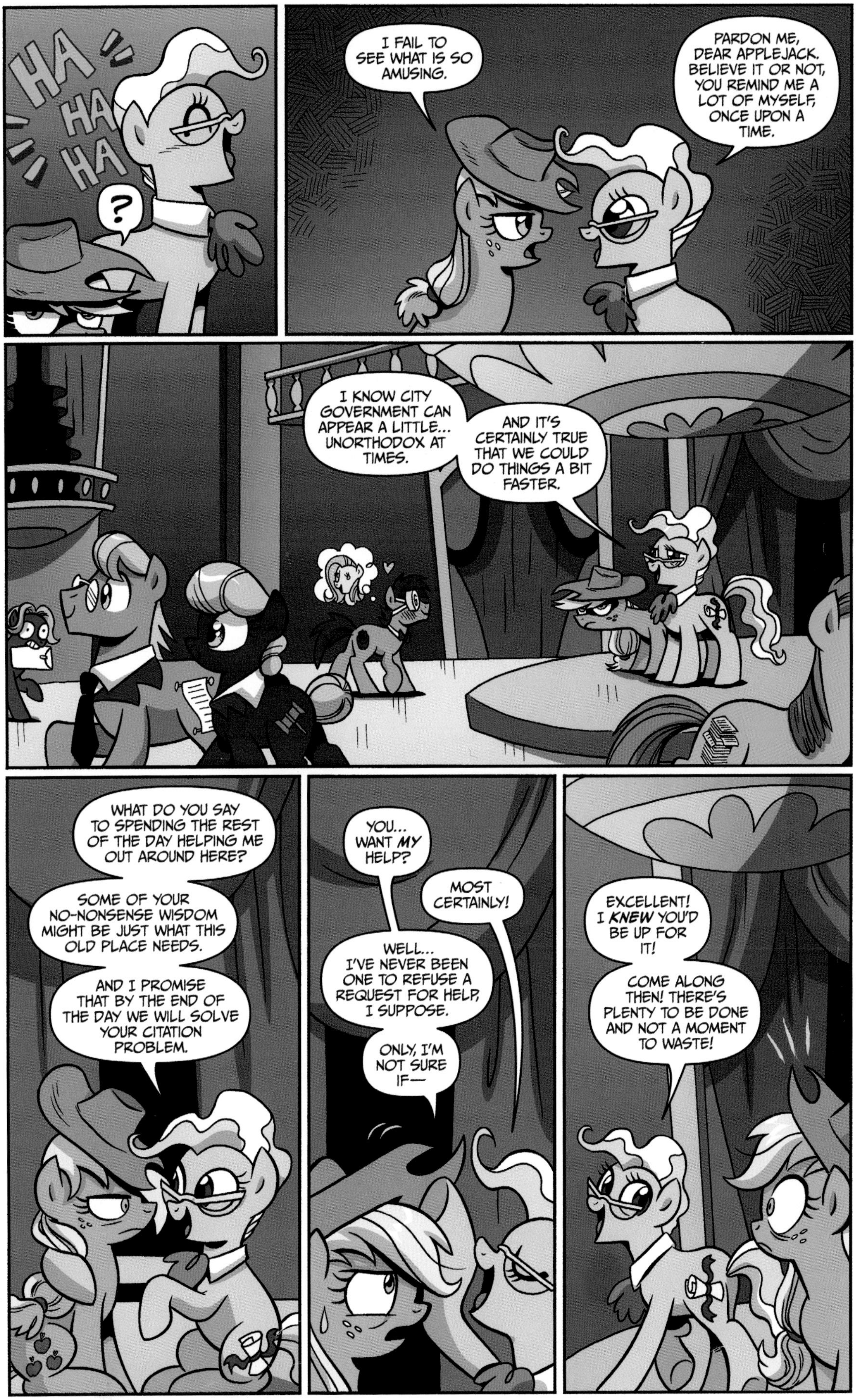
HA HA HA
?
I FAIL TO SEE WHAT IS SO AMUSING.
PARDON ME, DEAR APPLEJACK. BELIEVE IT OR NOT, YOU REMIND ME A LOT OF MYSELF, ONCE UPON A TIME.
I KNOW CITY GOVERNMENT CAN APPEAR A LITTLE... UNORTHODOX AT TIMES.
AND IT'S CERTAINLY TRUE THAT WE COULD DO THINGS A BIT FASTER.
WHAT DO YOU SAY TO SPENDING THE REST OF THE DAY HELPING ME OUT AROUND HERE?
SOME OF YOUR NO-NONSENSE WISDOM MIGHT BE JUST WHAT THIS OLD PLACE NEEDS.
AND I PROMISE THAT BY THE END OF THE DAY WE WILL SOLVE YOUR CITATION PROBLEM.
YOU... WANT *MY* HELP?
MOST CERTAINLY!
WELL... I'VE NEVER BEEN ONE TO REFUSE A REQUEST FOR HELP, I SUPPOSE.
ONLY, I'M NOT SURE IF—
EXCELLENT! I ***KNEW*** YOU'D BE UP FOR IT!
COME ALONG THEN! THERE'S PLENTY TO BE DONE AND NOT A MOMENT TO WASTE!

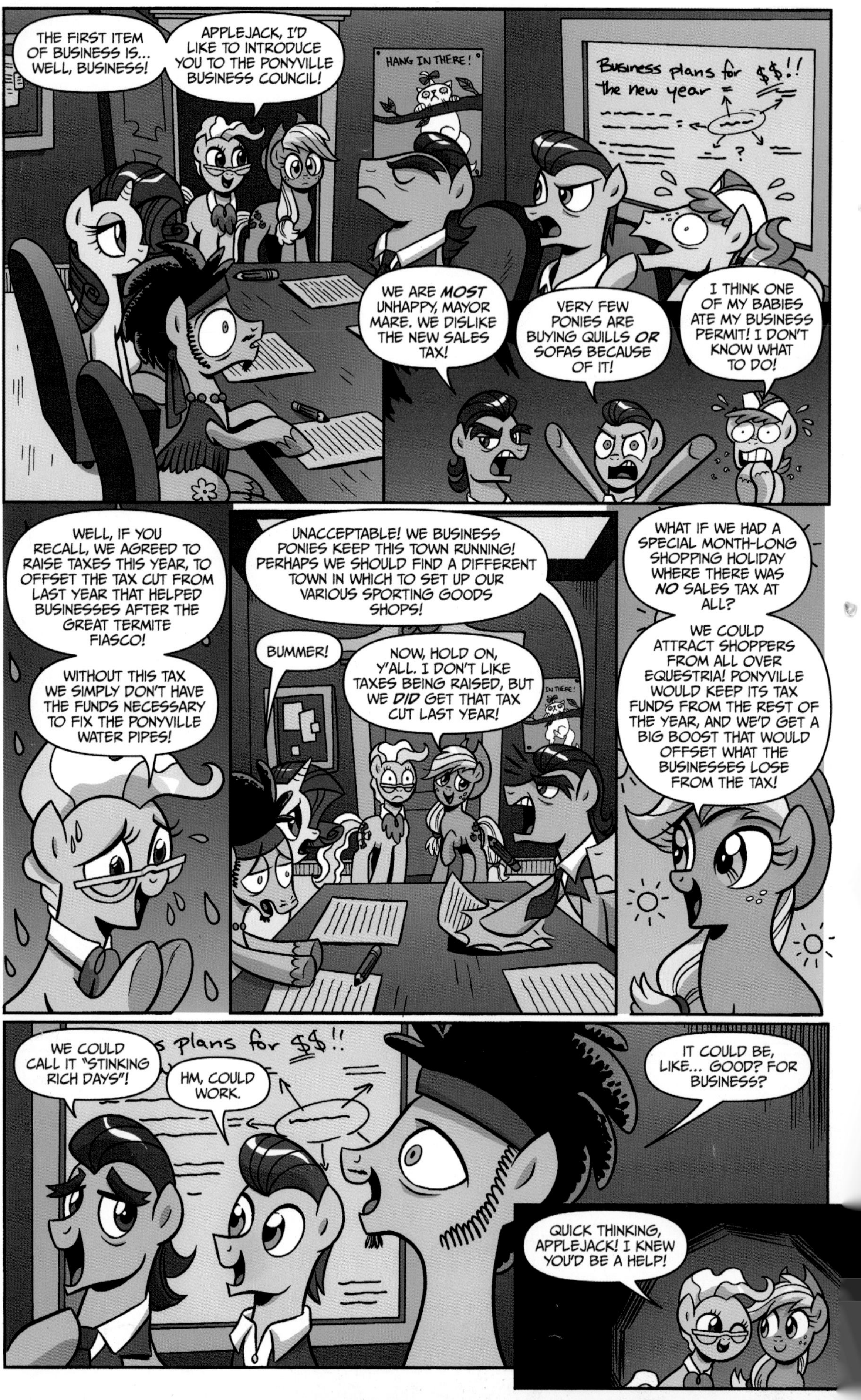

THE FIRST ITEM OF BUSINESS IS... WELL, BUSINESS!
APPLEJACK, I'D LIKE TO INTRODUCE YOU TO THE PONYVILLE BUSINESS COUNCIL!
HANG IN THERE!
Business plans for $$!! the new year
WE ARE *MOST* UNHAPPY, MAYOR MARE. WE DISLIKE THE NEW SALES TAX!
VERY FEW PONIES ARE BUYING QUILLS *OR* SOFAS BECAUSE OF IT!
I THINK ONE OF MY BABIES ATE MY BUSINESS PERMIT! I DON'T KNOW WHAT TO DO!
WELL, IF YOU RECALL, WE AGREED TO RAISE TAXES THIS YEAR, TO OFFSET THE TAX CUT FROM LAST YEAR THAT HELPED BUSINESSES AFTER THE GREAT TERMITE FIASCO!
WITHOUT THIS TAX WE SIMPLY DON'T HAVE THE FUNDS NECESSARY TO FIX THE PONYVILLE WATER PIPES!
UNACCEPTABLE! WE BUSINESS PONIES KEEP THIS TOWN RUNNING! PERHAPS WE SHOULD FIND A DIFFERENT TOWN IN WHICH TO SET UP OUR VARIOUS SPORTING GOODS SHOPS!
BUMMER!
NOW, HOLD ON, Y'ALL. I DON'T LIKE TAXES BEING RAISED, BUT WE *DID* GET THAT TAX CUT LAST YEAR!
IN THERE!
WHAT IF WE HAD A SPECIAL MONTH-LONG SHOPPING HOLIDAY WHERE THERE WAS *NO* SALES TAX AT ALL?
WE COULD ATTRACT SHOPPERS FROM ALL OVER EQUESTRIA! PONYVILLE WOULD KEEP ITS TAX FUNDS FROM THE REST OF THE YEAR, AND WE'D GET A BIG BOOST THAT WOULD OFFSET WHAT THE BUSINESSES LOSE FROM THE TAX!
WE COULD CALL IT "STINKING RICH DAYS"!
HM, COULD WORK.
s plans for $$!!
IT COULD BE, LIKE... GOOD? FOR BUSINESS?
QUICK THINKING, APPLEJACK! I KNEW YOU'D BE A HELP!

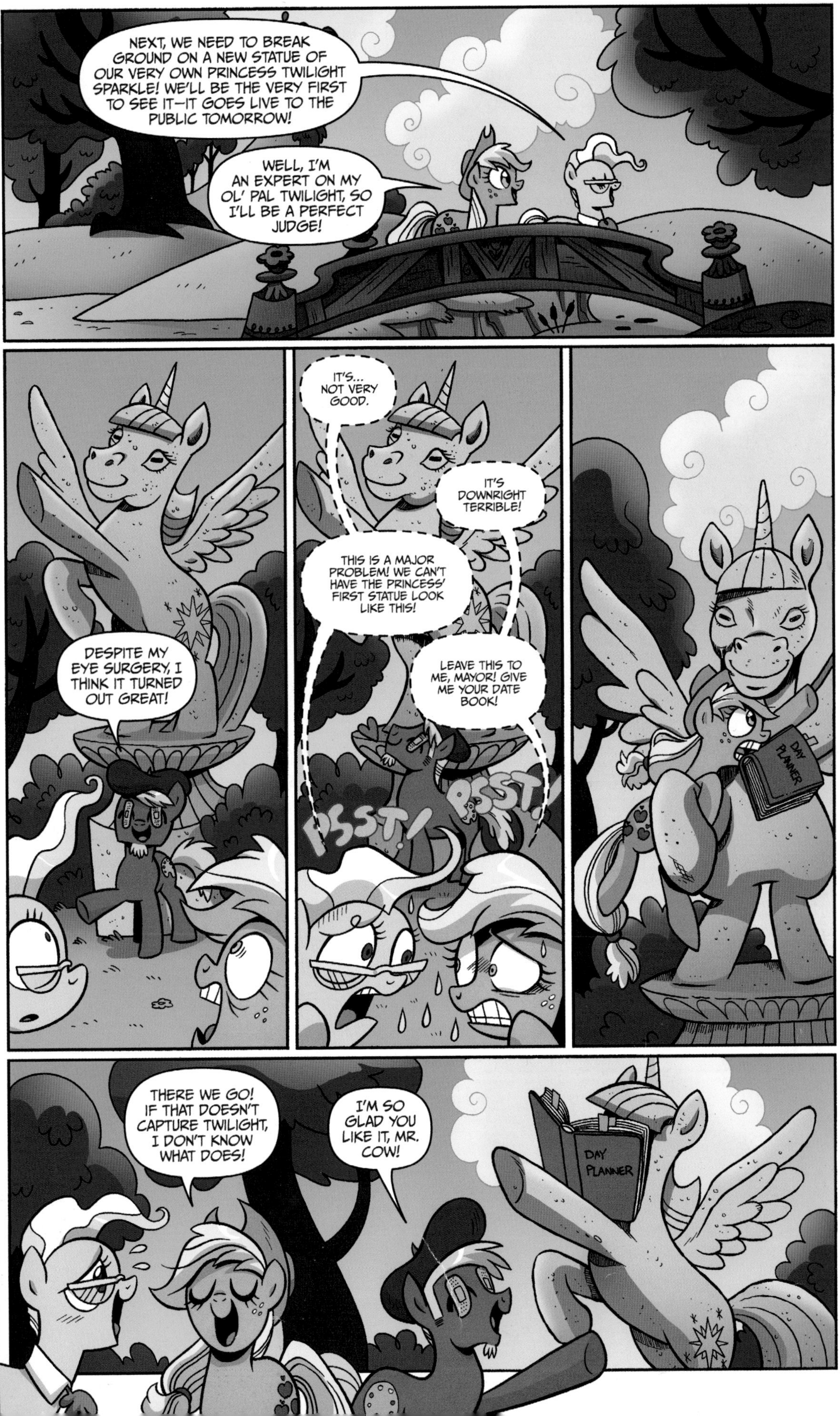
NEXT, WE NEED TO BREAK GROUND ON A NEW STATUE OF OUR VERY OWN PRINCESS TWILIGHT SPARKLE! WE'LL BE THE VERY FIRST TO SEE IT—IT GOES LIVE TO THE PUBLIC TOMORROW!
WELL, I'M AN EXPERT ON MY OL' PAL TWILIGHT, SO I'LL BE A PERFECT JUDGE!
DESPITE MY EYE SURGERY, I THINK IT TURNED OUT GREAT!
IT'S... NOT VERY GOOD.
IT'S DOWNRIGHT TERRIBLE!
THIS IS A MAJOR PROBLEM! WE CAN'T HAVE THE PRINCESS' FIRST STATUE LOOK LIKE THIS!
LEAVE THIS TO ME, MAYOR! GIVE ME YOUR DATE BOOK!
PSST!
PSST!
DAY PLANNER
THERE WE GO! IF THAT DOESN'T CAPTURE TWILIGHT, I DON'T KNOW WHAT DOES!
I'M SO GLAD YOU LIKE IT, MR. COW!
DAY PLANNER

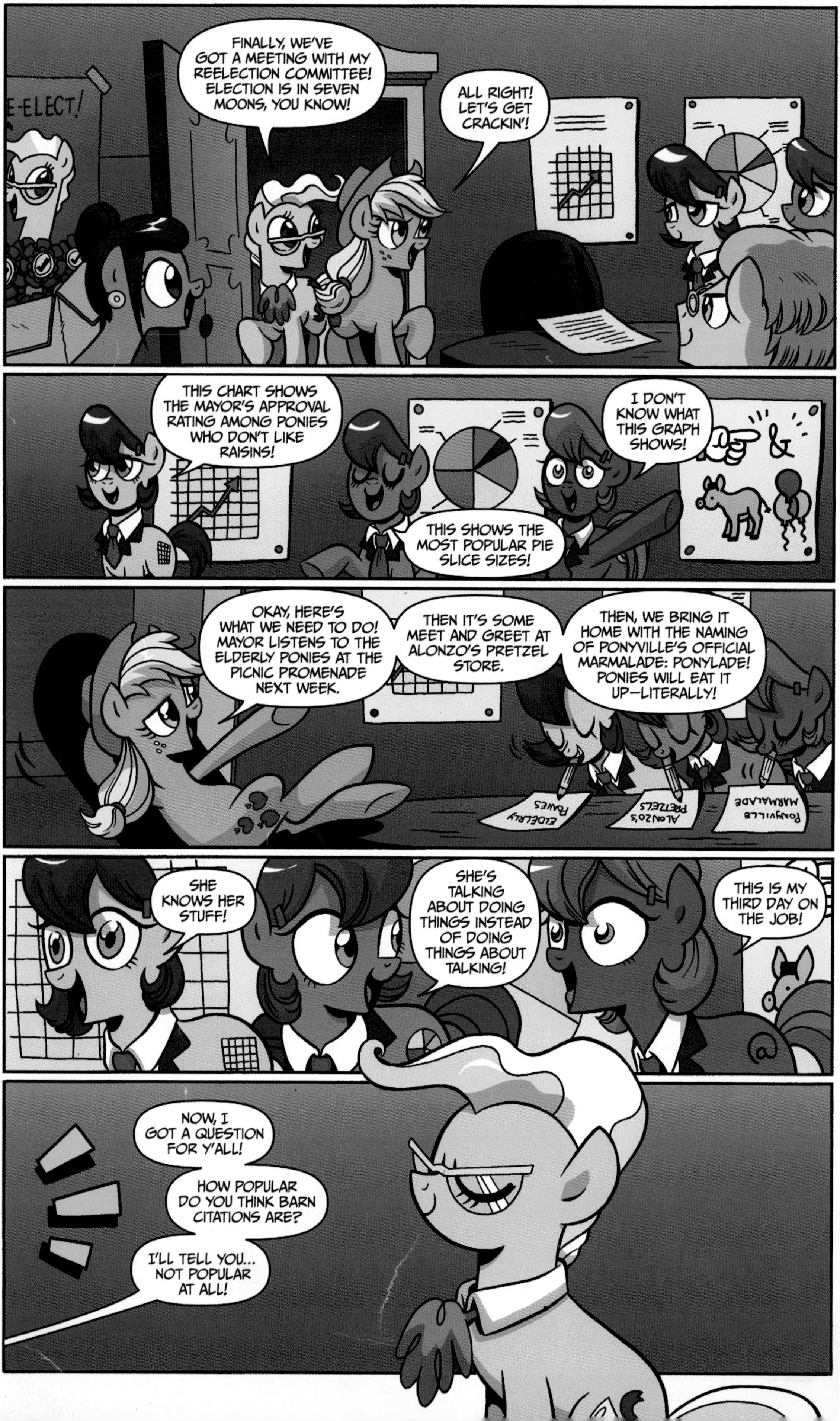
FINALLY, WE'VE GOT A MEETING WITH MY REELECTION COMMITTEE! ELECTION IS IN SEVEN MOONS, YOU KNOW!
ALL RIGHT! LET'S GET CRACKIN'!
THIS CHART SHOWS THE MAYOR'S APPROVAL RATING AMONG PONIES WHO DON'T LIKE RAISINS!
THIS SHOWS THE MOST POPULAR PIE SLICE SIZES!
I DON'T KNOW WHAT THIS GRAPH SHOWS!
OKAY, HERE'S WHAT WE NEED TO DO! MAYOR LISTENS TO THE ELDERLY PONIES AT THE PICNIC PROMENADE NEXT WEEK.
THEN IT'S SOME MEET AND GREET AT ALONZO'S PRETZEL STORE.
THEN, WE BRING IT HOME WITH THE NAMING OF PONYVILLE'S OFFICIAL MARMALADE: PONYLADE! PONIES WILL EAT IT UP—LITERALLY!
ELDERLY PONIES
ALONZO'S PRETZELS
PONYVILLE MARMALADE
SHE KNOWS HER STUFF!
SHE'S TALKING ABOUT DOING THINGS INSTEAD OF DOING THINGS ABOUT TALKING!
THIS IS MY THIRD DAY ON THE JOB!
NOW, I GOT A QUESTION FOR Y'ALL!
HOW POPULAR DO YOU THINK BARN CITATIONS ARE?
I'LL TELL YOU... NOT POPULAR AT ALL!

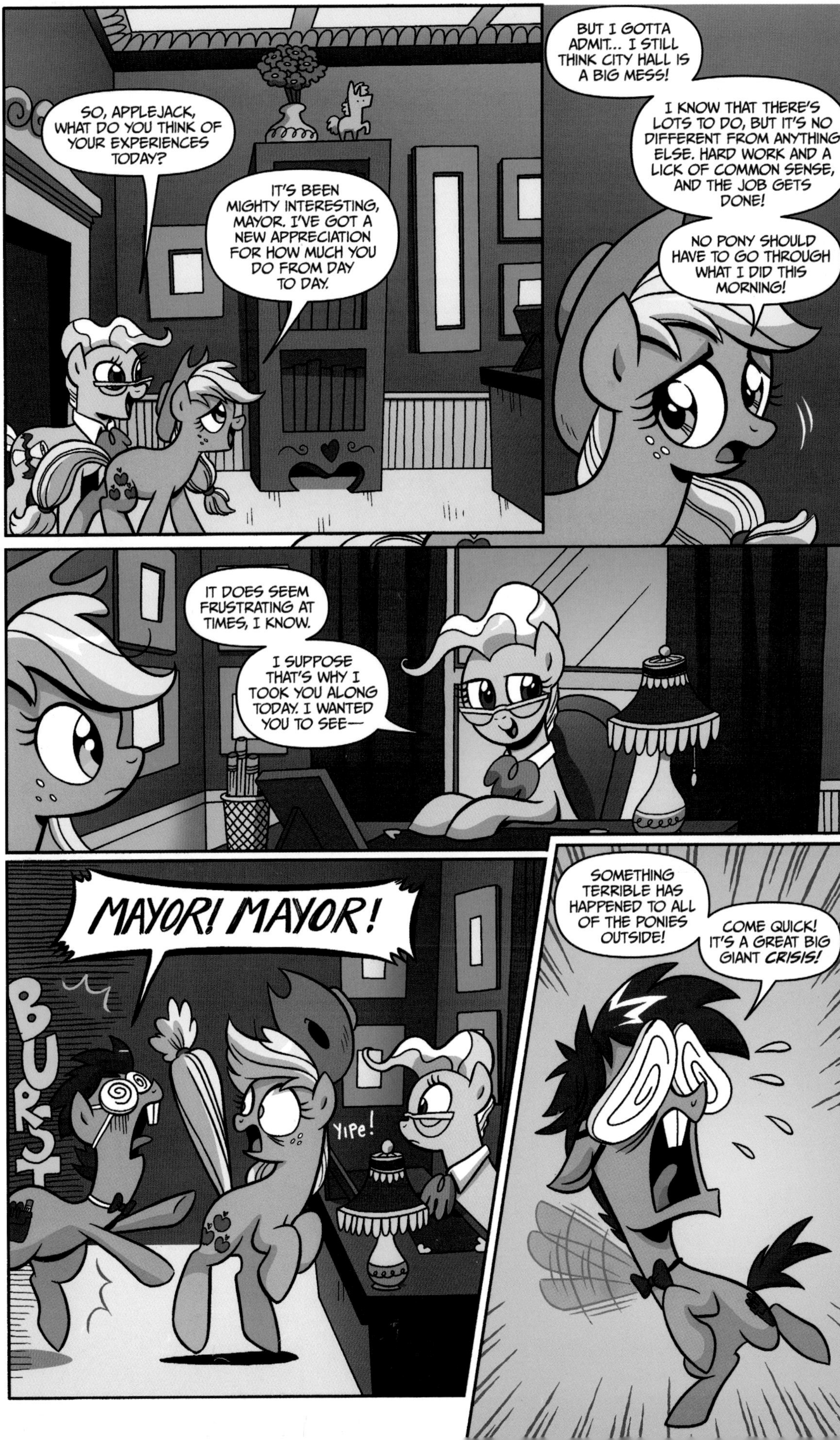
SO, APPLEJACK, WHAT DO YOU THINK OF YOUR EXPERIENCES TODAY?
IT'S BEEN MIGHTY INTERESTING, MAYOR. I'VE GOT A NEW APPRECIATION FOR HOW MUCH YOU DO FROM DAY TO DAY.
BUT I GOTTA ADMIT... I STILL THINK CITY HALL IS A BIG MESS!
I KNOW THAT THERE'S LOTS TO DO, BUT IT'S NO DIFFERENT FROM ANYTHING ELSE. HARD WORK AND A LICK OF COMMON SENSE, AND THE JOB GETS DONE!
NO PONY SHOULD HAVE TO GO THROUGH WHAT I DID THIS MORNING!
IT DOES SEEM FRUSTRATING AT TIMES, I KNOW.
I SUPPOSE THAT'S WHY I TOOK YOU ALONG TODAY. I WANTED YOU TO SEE—
MAYOR! MAYOR!
BURST
YIPE!
SOMETHING TERRIBLE HAS HAPPENED TO ALL OF THE PONIES OUTSIDE!
COME QUICK! IT'S A GREAT BIG GIANT CRISIS!

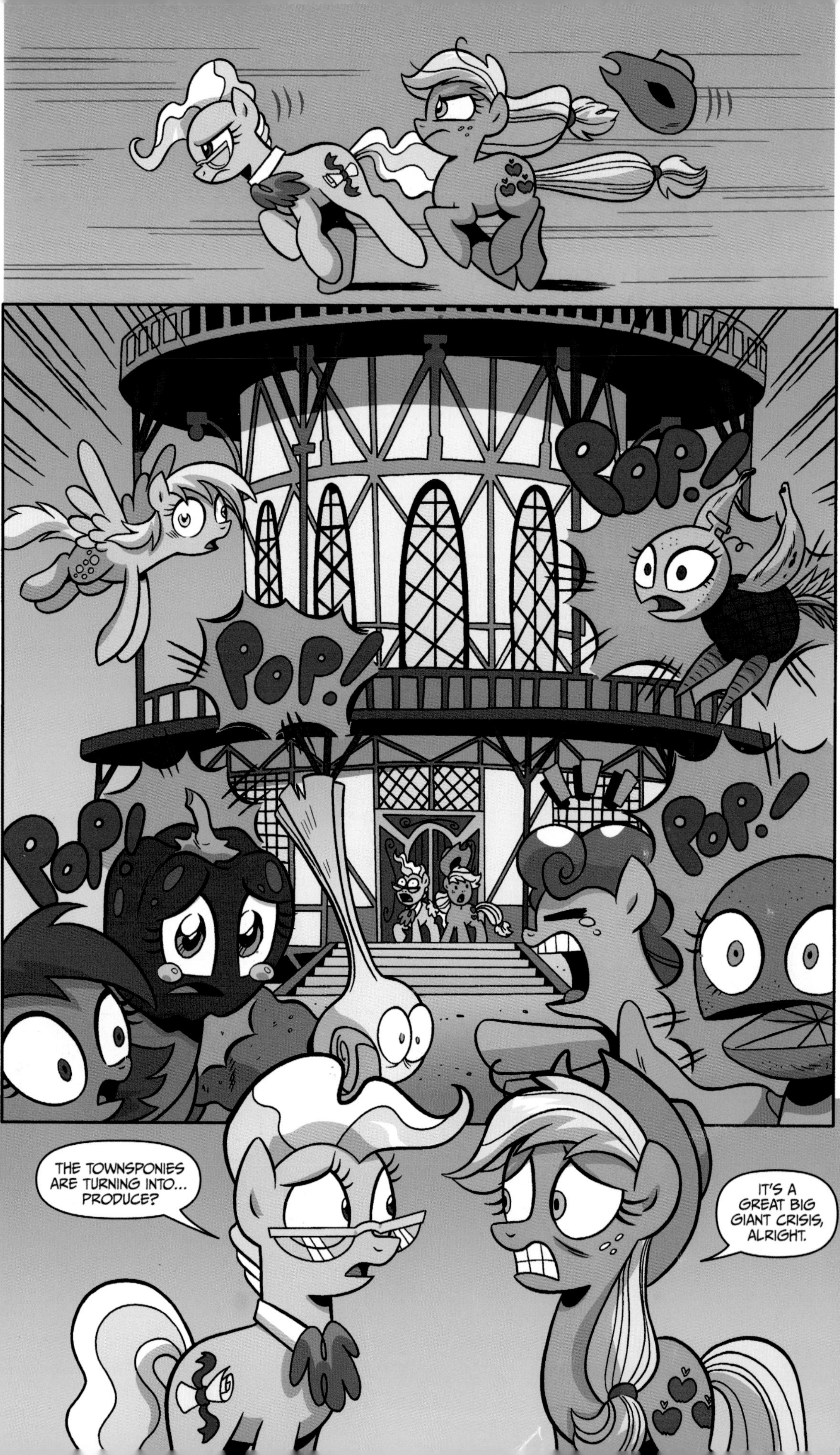
POP!
POP!
POP!
POP!
THE TOWNSPONIES ARE TURNING INTO... PRODUCE?
IT'S A GREAT BIG GIANT CRISIS, ALRIGHT.

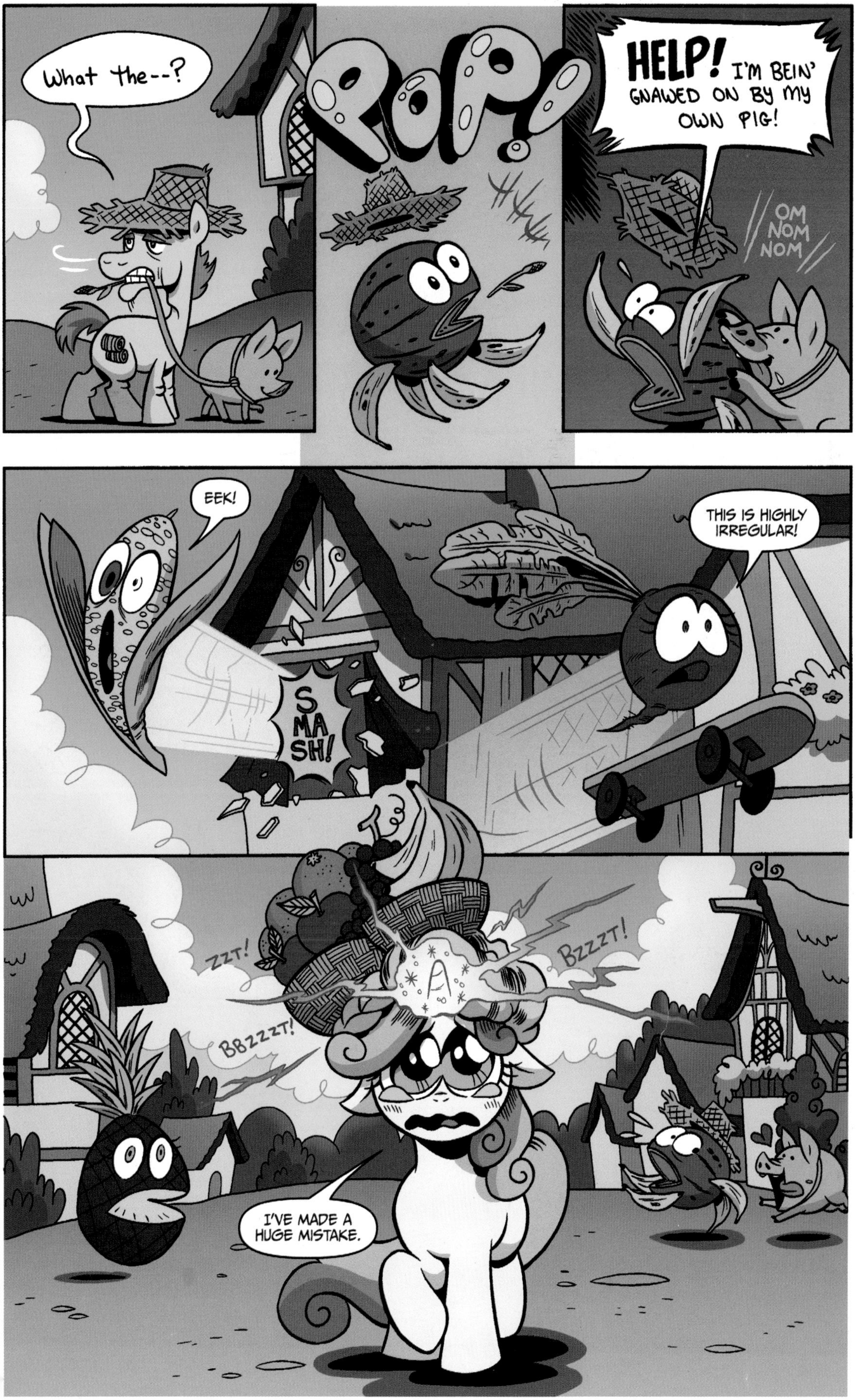
What the--?
POP!
HELP! I'M BEIN' GNAWED ON BY MY OWN PIG!
OM NOM NOM
EEK!
SMASH!
THIS IS HIGHLY IRREGULAR!
ZZT!
BZZZT!
BBZZZT!
I'VE MADE A HUGE MISTAKE.

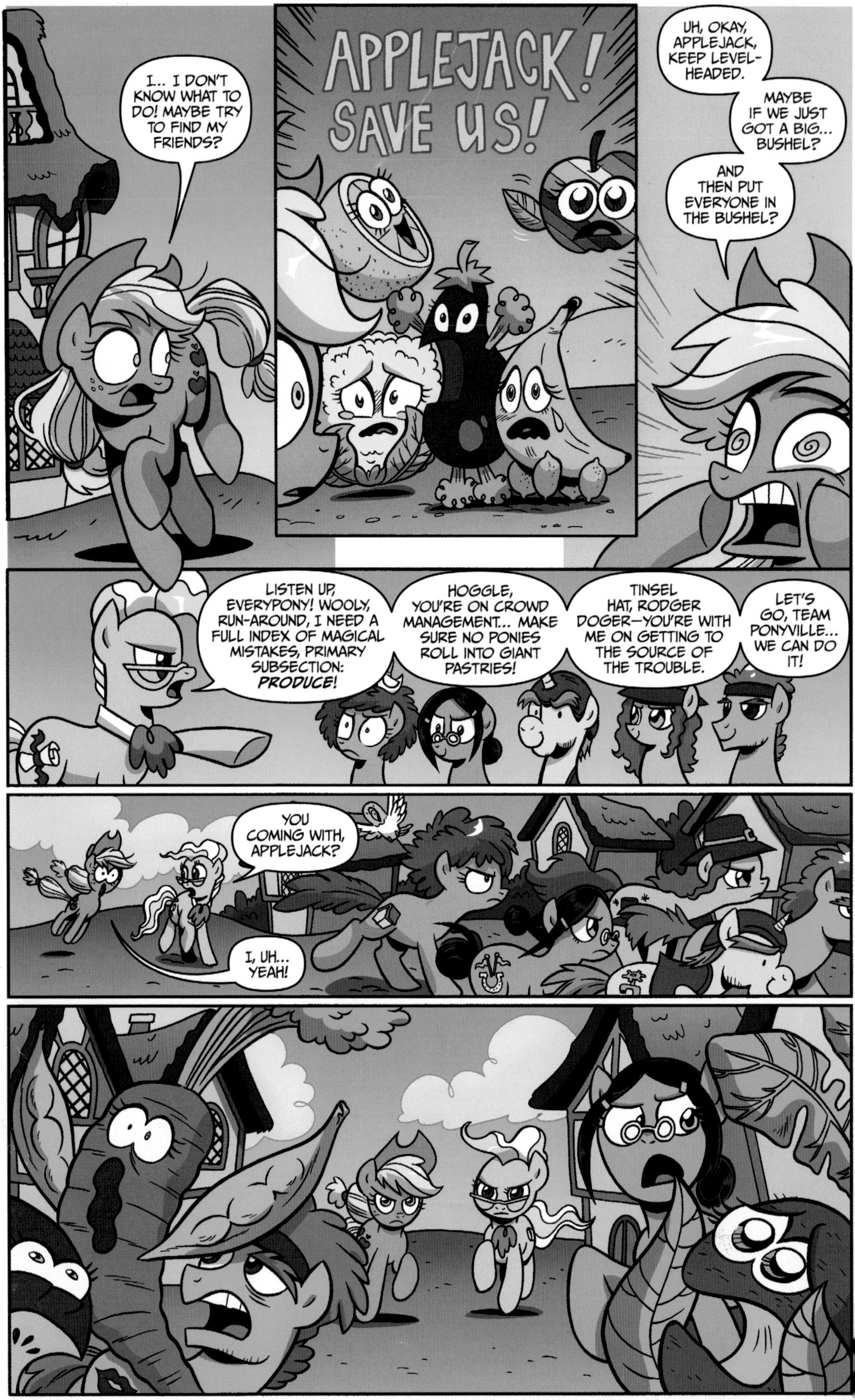
I... I DON'T KNOW WHAT TO DO! MAYBE TRY TO FIND MY FRIENDS?
APPLEJACK! SAVE US!
UH, OKAY, APPLEJACK, KEEP LEVEL-HEADED.
MAYBE IF WE JUST GOT A BIG... BUSHEL?
AND THEN PUT EVERYONE IN THE BUSHEL?
LISTEN UP, EVERYPONY! WOOLY, RUN-AROUND, I NEED A FULL INDEX OF MAGICAL MISTAKES, PRIMARY SUBSECTION: *PRODUCE*!
HOGGLE, YOU'RE ON CROWD MANAGEMENT... MAKE SURE NO PONIES ROLL INTO GIANT PASTRIES!
TINSEL HAT, RODGER DOGER—YOU'RE WITH ME ON GETTING TO THE SOURCE OF THE TROUBLE.
LET'S GO, TEAM PONYVILLE... WE CAN DO IT!
YOU COMING WITH, APPLEJACK?
I, UH... YEAH!

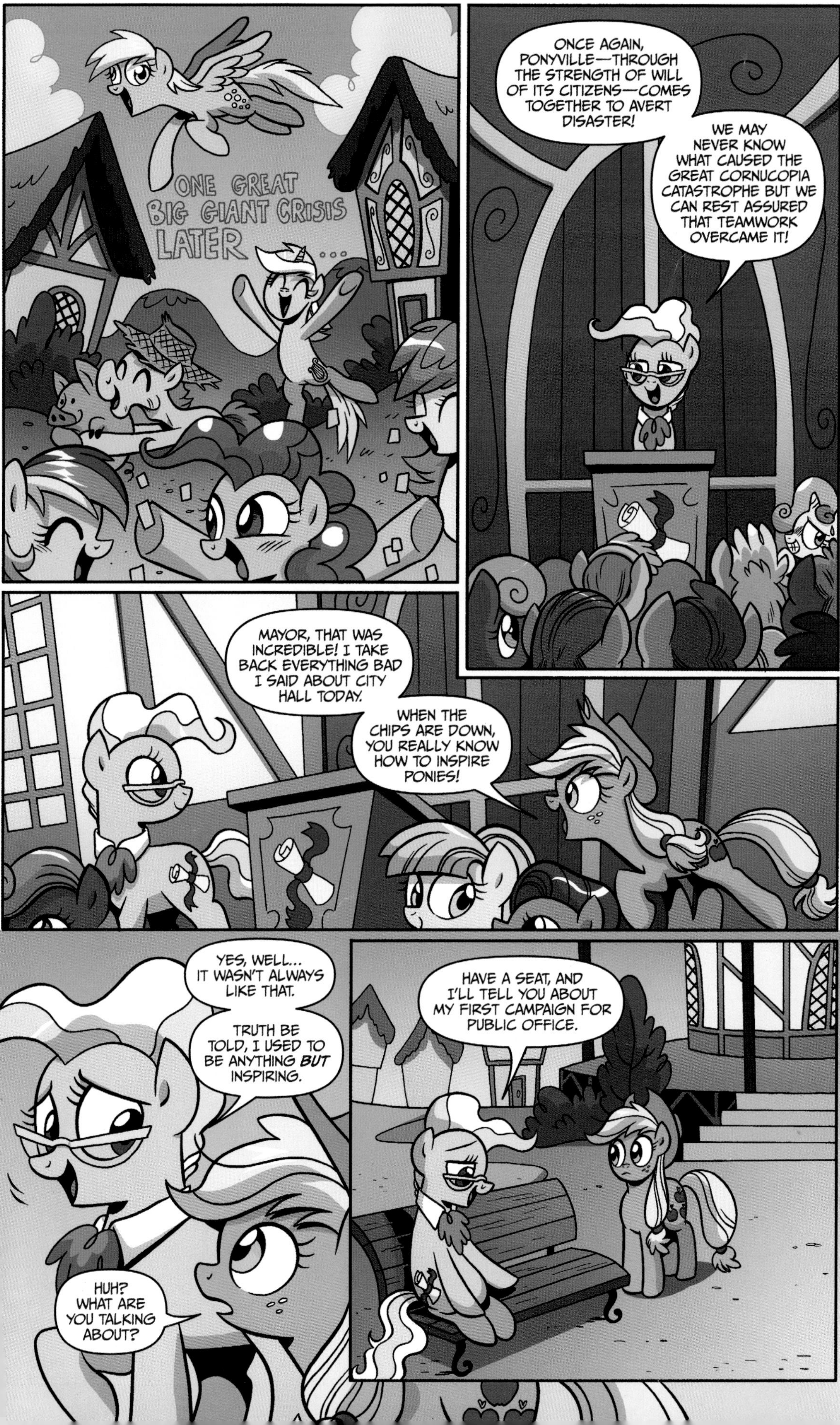
ONE GREAT BIG GIANT CRISIS LATER...
ONCE AGAIN, PONYVILLE—THROUGH THE STRENGTH OF WILL OF ITS CITIZENS—COMES TOGETHER TO AVERT DISASTER!
WE MAY NEVER KNOW WHAT CAUSED THE GREAT CORNUCOPIA CATASTROPHE BUT WE CAN REST ASSURED THAT TEAMWORK OVERCAME IT!
MAYOR, THAT WAS INCREDIBLE! I TAKE BACK EVERYTHING BAD I SAID ABOUT CITY HALL TODAY.
WHEN THE CHIPS ARE DOWN, YOU REALLY KNOW HOW TO INSPIRE PONIES!
YES, WELL... IT WASN'T ALWAYS LIKE THAT.
TRUTH BE TOLD, I USED TO BE ANYTHING *BUT* INSPIRING.
HUH? WHAT ARE YOU TALKING ABOUT?
HAVE A SEAT, AND I'LL TELL YOU ABOUT MY FIRST CAMPAIGN FOR PUBLIC OFFICE.

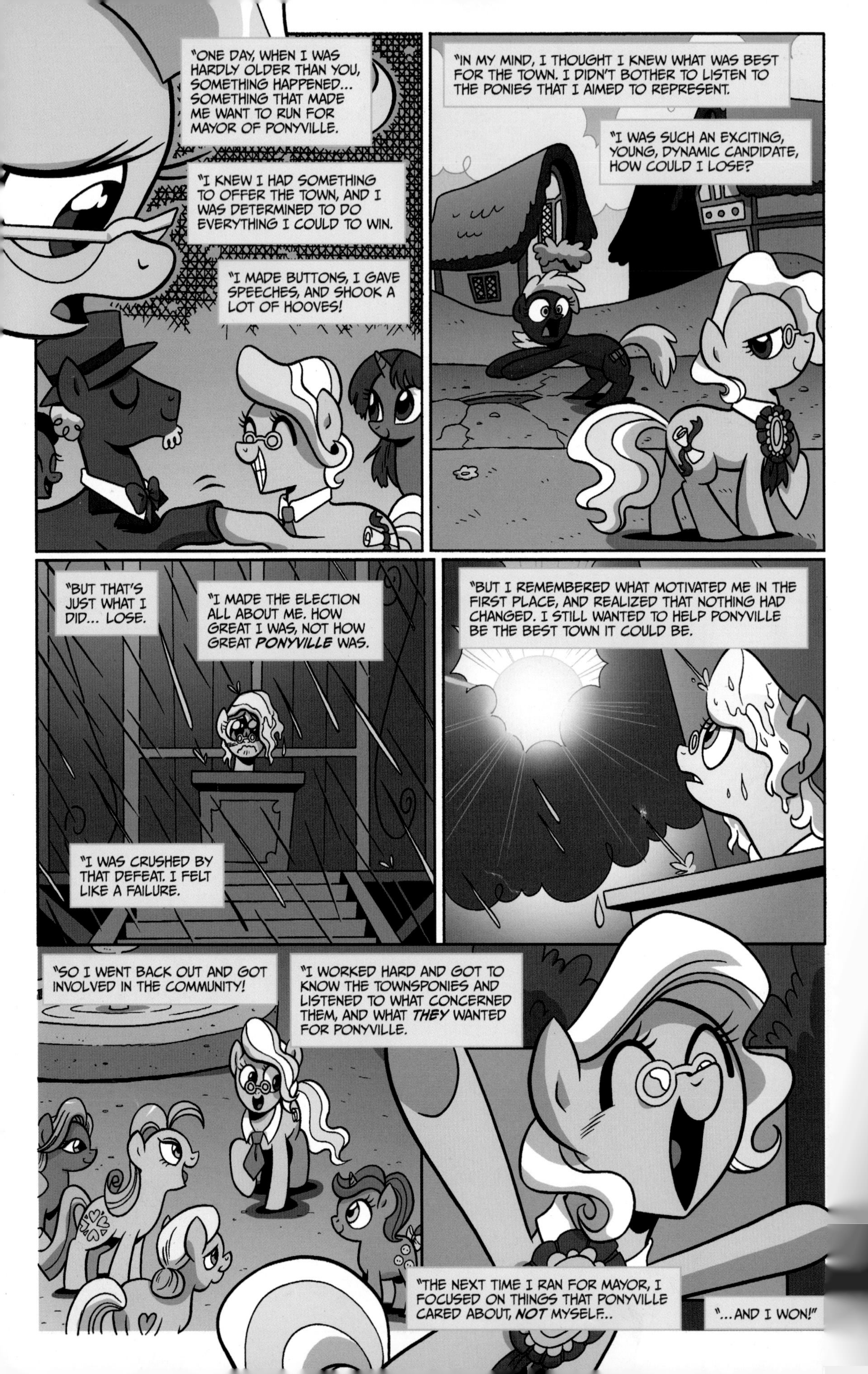
"ONE DAY, WHEN I WAS HARDLY OLDER THAN YOU, SOMETHING HAPPENED... SOMETHING THAT MADE ME WANT TO RUN FOR MAYOR OF PONYVILLE.
"I KNEW I HAD SOMETHING TO OFFER THE TOWN, AND I WAS DETERMINED TO DO EVERYTHING I COULD TO WIN.
"I MADE BUTTONS, I GAVE SPEECHES, AND SHOOK A LOT OF HOOVES!
"IN MY MIND, I THOUGHT I KNEW WHAT WAS BEST FOR THE TOWN. I DIDN'T BOTHER TO LISTEN TO THE PONIES THAT I AIMED TO REPRESENT.
"I WAS SUCH AN EXCITING, YOUNG, DYNAMIC CANDIDATE, HOW COULD I LOSE?
"BUT THAT'S JUST WHAT I DID... LOSE.
"I MADE THE ELECTION ALL ABOUT ME. HOW GREAT I WAS, NOT HOW GREAT *PONYVILLE* WAS.
"I WAS CRUSHED BY THAT DEFEAT. I FELT LIKE A FAILURE.
"BUT I REMEMBERED WHAT MOTIVATED ME IN THE FIRST PLACE, AND REALIZED THAT NOTHING HAD CHANGED. I STILL WANTED TO HELP PONYVILLE BE THE BEST TOWN IT COULD BE.
"SO I WENT BACK OUT AND GOT INVOLVED IN THE COMMUNITY!
"I WORKED HARD AND GOT TO KNOW THE TOWNSPONIES AND LISTENED TO WHAT CONCERNED THEM, AND WHAT *THEY* WANTED FOR PONYVILLE.
"THE NEXT TIME I RAN FOR MAYOR, I FOCUSED ON THINGS THAT PONYVILLE CARED ABOUT, *NOT* MYSELF...
"...AND I WON!"

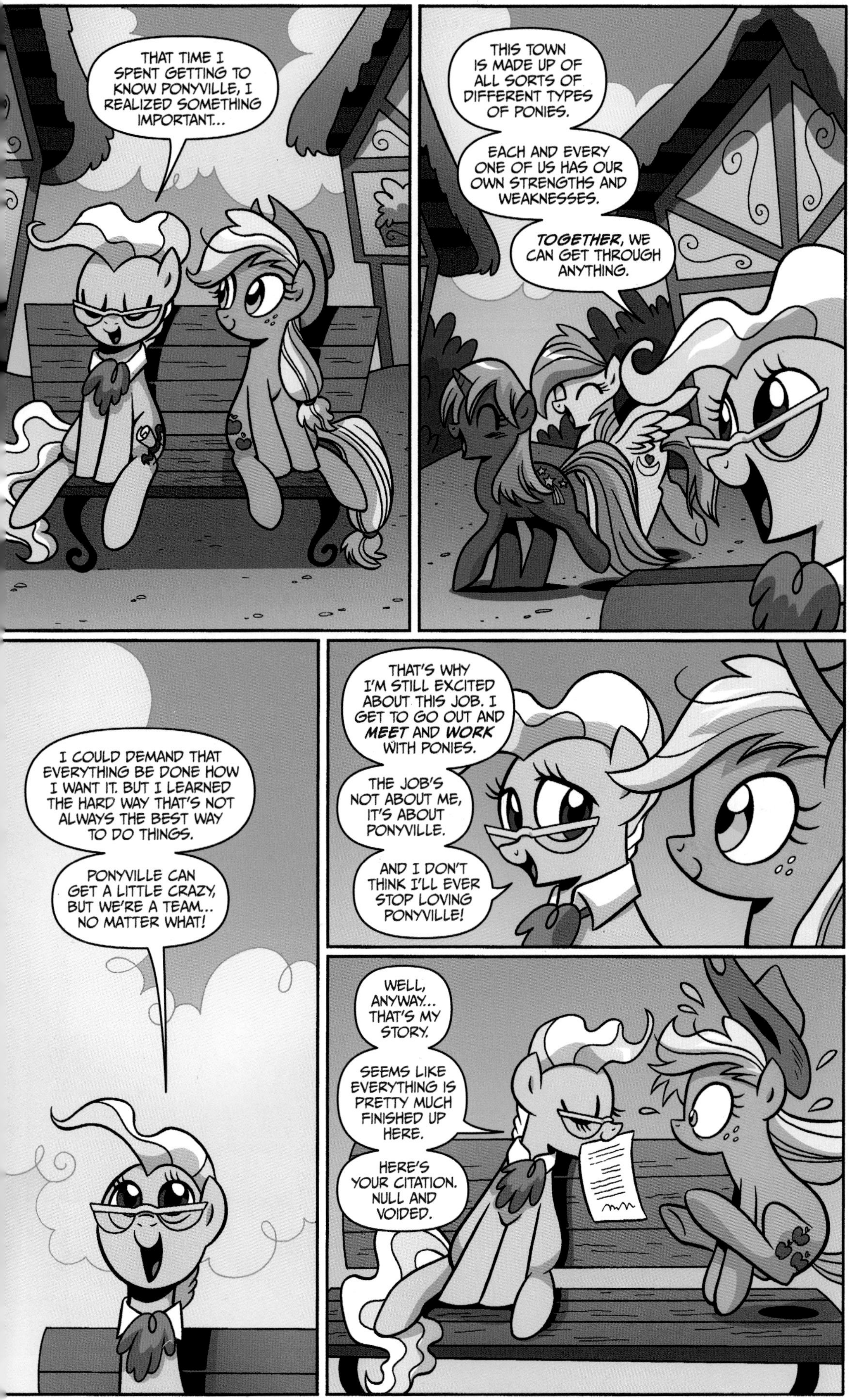
THAT TIME I SPENT GETTING TO KNOW PONYVILLE, I REALIZED SOMETHING IMPORTANT...
THIS TOWN IS MADE UP OF ALL SORTS OF DIFFERENT TYPES OF PONIES.
EACH AND EVERY ONE OF US HAS OUR OWN STRENGTHS AND WEAKNESSES.
TOGETHER, WE CAN GET THROUGH ANYTHING.
I COULD DEMAND THAT EVERYTHING BE DONE HOW I WANT IT. BUT I LEARNED THE HARD WAY THAT'S NOT ALWAYS THE BEST WAY TO DO THINGS.
PONYVILLE CAN GET A LITTLE CRAZY, BUT WE'RE A TEAM... NO MATTER WHAT!
THAT'S WHY I'M STILL EXCITED ABOUT THIS JOB. I GET TO GO OUT AND MEET AND WORK WITH PONIES.
THE JOB'S NOT ABOUT ME, IT'S ABOUT PONYVILLE.
AND I DON'T THINK I'LL EVER STOP LOVING PONYVILLE!
WELL, ANYWAY... THAT'S MY STORY.
SEEMS LIKE EVERYTHING IS PRETTY MUCH FINISHED UP HERE.
HERE'S YOUR CITATION. NULL AND VOIDED.

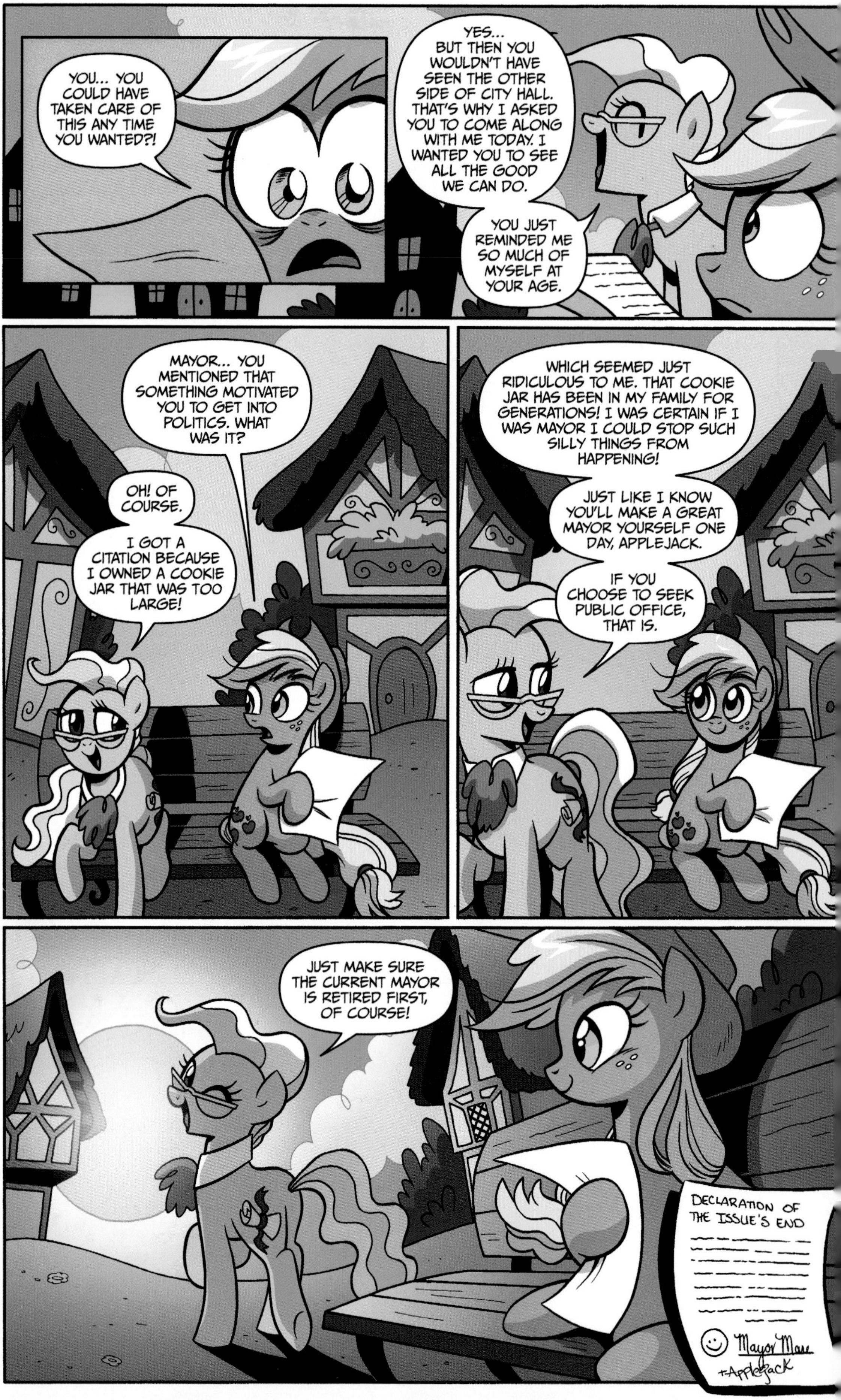

YOU... YOU COULD HAVE TAKEN CARE OF THIS ANY TIME YOU WANTED?!
YES... BUT THEN YOU WOULDN'T HAVE SEEN THE OTHER SIDE OF CITY HALL. THAT'S WHY I ASKED YOU TO COME ALONG WITH ME TODAY. I WANTED YOU TO SEE ALL THE GOOD WE CAN DO.
YOU JUST REMINDED ME SO MUCH OF MYSELF AT YOUR AGE.
MAYOR... YOU MENTIONED THAT SOMETHING MOTIVATED YOU TO GET INTO POLITICS. WHAT WAS IT?
OH! OF COURSE.
I GOT A CITATION BECAUSE I OWNED A COOKIE JAR THAT WAS TOO LARGE!
WHICH SEEMED JUST RIDICULOUS TO ME. THAT COOKIE JAR HAS BEEN IN MY FAMILY FOR GENERATIONS! I WAS CERTAIN IF I WAS MAYOR I COULD STOP SUCH SILLY THINGS FROM HAPPENING!
JUST LIKE I KNOW YOU'LL MAKE A GREAT MAYOR YOURSELF ONE DAY, APPLEJACK.
IF YOU CHOOSE TO SEEK PUBLIC OFFICE, THAT IS.
JUST MAKE SURE THE CURRENT MAYOR IS RETIRED FIRST, OF COURSE!
DECLARATION OF THE ISSUE'S END
Mayor Mare
+Applejack